FATAL LUCK

By

Dorothy Howell

D1519866

Dorothy Howell

ISBN: 978-0-9856930-3-9
Published in the United States of America

Fatal Luck

—

DEDICATION:
To all my loved ones for their endless support

ACKNOWLEDGMENT:
I couldn't have written this novella without the help of many people. Some of them are: Judith Branstetter, Stacy Howell, Evie Cook, the gifted folks at Webcrafters Design, and William F. Wu, Ph.D.

BOOK LIST:

Books by Dorothy Howell

The Haley Randolph Mystery Series

Handbags and Homicide
Purses and Poison
Shoulder Bags and Shootings
Clutches and Curses
Tote Bags and Toe Tags
Evening Bags and Executions
Beach Bags and Burglaries

The Dana Mackenzie Mystery Series

Fatal Debt
Fatal Luck

Fatal Luck

By

Dorothy Howell

Dorothy Howell

Chapter 1

Sometimes you get lucky.

I'm not talking about sex—although that topic came up often. No, I'm talking about actual luck, good luck—kismet, serendipity, the fortuitous alignment of the planets. Thankfully, my mojo was working pretty well because it kept me from witnessing a murder.

Not bad for a Monday morning.

I'm Dana Mackenzie. I worked for Mid-America Financial Services, a nationwide consumer finance company that granted personal loans, home equity mortgages, and some dealer financing for things like TVs, stereos, and furniture.

Mid-America made loans to just about anybody for just about anything. The tricky part wasn't lending out the money, of course, it was collecting it back. That's where I came in.

A lot of people thought this was not a good way for a 27-year-old single female to spend her days. Sometimes, I agreed.

Mid-America had about a thousand branch offices nationwide, one of which was located a few miles away in Santa Flores where I worked. Another was here in Bonita, a city that adjoined Santa Flores, where I was starting my Monday morning. Like most of Southern California, the two cities melted into each other, indistinguishable except for lines drawn on a map.

The Bonita branch was located in a strip mall that

housed an insurance office, a hair salon, a gift shop, a deli, and four empty storefronts. I stopped by as needed to pick up real estate appraisal reports on my way into the office that I called home for eight-plus hours a day, down on Fifth Street.

I could have gone straight into the insurance office where the appraiser, an old guy named Jerry Donavan, rented a tiny space, but I was acquainted with everyone who worked in Mid-America's Bonita branch, and it would be rude not stop in and say hello.

Besides, I could get a coffee there and it was a good reason to keep from going to my own branch.

I swung into the alley behind the Bonita branch on State Street, parked, and got out. A little early morning sunlight seeped through the overcast November sky, giving the air a crisp autumn feel—or at least the closest we here in Southern California got to it—making it perfect weather for the pants, blouse and blazer I had on.

Employees of the Bonita branch groused about the location of their office—which had been selected by a guy in our home office in Chicago using a Google images search, apparently. In yet another flash of corporate brilliance, the strip mall on State Street, a major artery in the area, had been selected because of its signage and accessibility. Nobody bothered to look at the rear of the property, however.

The employee parking lot was small, separated from the rear of the building by a narrow alley that ran the length of the strip mall. The one security light offered little illumination, and the two Dumpsters drew scavengers and the homeless. A tall block wall covered with graffiti separated the parking lot from an apartment complex known for drug activity.

Leave it to Corporate.

The rear door to the Mid-America office was propped open a few inches, so I walked inside. With drug dealers in the area and questionable people roaming the alley, you'd think they'd keep the door locked.

I guess the branch manager thought that if employees faced a locked door in the morning, they might turn around and go back home.

Maybe he had a point.

The rear entrance led into the office's stock room which was filled with shelves of supplies and boxes of old documents; the restroom and a break room were off to the left. The door that led into the office stood open. The corporate decorator had played it fast and loose, painting the walls off-white, throwing down beige carpet, and selecting neutral colored desks and chairs.

Gloria Colton, the branch assistant manager, poked her head out of the break room.

"Oh. Dana. It's just you," she mumbled, then disappeared again.

Gloria had to be in her late thirties but already looked as if she were losing the battle against aging. Short, round everywhere, with hair that resembled a bale of hay and skin similar in texture to an American Tourister carry-on, she looked as if she'd attempted every beauty treatment known to womankind, and each and every one had failed.

Gloria was a bit of a failure herself, from the rumors I'd heard. She'd been with Mid-America for over ten years and had been repeatedly passed over for promotion to branch manager. She'd transferred to branch after branch all over Southern California and, somehow, she'd landed here at the Bonita office a few months ago.

I tried to like her, but the best I could do was tolerate her.

Gloria walked out of the break room with a steaming cup, passed me, and went into the office without speaking.

"I'll just have a quick cup of coffee," I called, to show her what good manners sounded like.

She didn't bother to look back.

It was much too early in the day to get annoyed, I decided. Besides, the coffee smelled great.

I stepped into the break room, a tiny place barely big enough for the table and four chairs, the mini-fridge, and the counter with a sink and microwave. It had the same look and smell of every other break room I'd been in. Coffee cup rings on the counter, cups and spoons that never seemed clean but were used anyway.

I found a mug in the cupboard and was reaching for the pot when I heard the roar of a car engine, followed by screaming.

I ran to the back door. Across the parking lot standing next to her car was Janine Ferris, the office's asset manager, screaming hysterically.

On the ground in the center of the alley lay an odd bundle of something. A few second passed before I realized it was a man.

"Call 9-1-1! Somebody got hit by a car in the alley!" I shouted to Gloria, and sprinted outside.

I rushed to the man lying on the pavement. Blood poured from what was left of his skull. I knew I couldn't do anything to help him.

I turned away and looked up and down the alley in both directions. No sign of the car that had hit him. Nobody had stopped, pulled over, gotten out. Whoever had done this had kept going.

—

Janine continued screaming. She'd gone white, yet her cheeks were flushed, her eyes wide with horror.

I jogged across the alley.

"Janine? Janine!" I said.

She kept shrieking.

My people skills aren't the best, and all I could think to do was to grab her shoulders and give her a little shake.

"Why! Oh, my God! Why would anybody do that!" She screamed the words in my face. "Oh, my God! Poor Jerry!"

"Jerry?"

I whipped back to the body in the alley. Bits of broken glass shimmered in the sunlight. A stack of blood soaked papers fluttered in the breeze. I tilted my head left, then right. The height and gray hair, the gut hanging over the belt looked familiar.

"Oh, my God," I mumbled. "Jerry."

Jerry Donavan, the appraiser I'd come here to meet.

I guess his mojo wasn't working at all this morning.

"Why! Oh, my God! Why would somebody do that!" Janine shrieked. "Deliberately run him over!"

I looked up and down the alley again. It flashed in my head that whoever had hit Jerry might have gone into some sort of shock, which was understandable, but would grasp reality in a minute or so, turn around and come back. But there was no sign of a car returning to the scene.

"Oh, my God!" Janine screamed. "How could somebody do that! Just run over somebody! Why would anybody want to kill him?"

Obviously, Janine didn't know Jerry Donavan as well as I did because I wondered just the opposite.

Why *wouldn't* somebody want to kill him?

Chapter 2

I got Janine, still screaming hysterically, into the break room. Gloria wandered in, poured a cup of coffee, and drank it herself.

"Janine, you have to calm down," I said, as loud as I could without screaming myself.

That only escalated her wailing. Incredibly, I heard sirens over her shrieks and made a move for the door, but Gloria beat me to it, leaving me stranded with screaming Janine.

Granted, my people skills are often lacking. I knew I couldn't leave her alone in her condition. But my ears had started to ring and she was getting on my nerves big-time. Just as I was seriously considering slapping her across the face—I'd always wanted to do that to someone—she clammed up.

Nick Travis walked into the break room.

He had that effect on a lot of women. Including me.

Nick was a homicide detective. He and I had history stretching back to high school here in Santa Flores when he was dating my best friend Katie Jo Miller and something ugly—really ugly—happened between them.

Nick seemed to think he and I had a future together, but we didn't. He refused to come clean about what happened back in high school, and I couldn't get past it.

Nick had been pursuing me for a while now, making his intentions obvious. He wants me. I know he does.

But I was standing on principle. Not always easy

where handsome, tall, broad-shouldered, dark haired, blue-eyed Nick Travis was concerned.

Thankfully, for once, Nick's good looks had worked in my favor. He'd snapped Janine out of her screaming fit with his mere presence.

"Let's sit down," Nick said, gesturing to the little table in the center of the break room.

His voice had a soothing effect, a lure nearly impossible to ignore. Like a Stepford wife, Janine moved to one of the chairs and sat down. I caught myself just in time and remained standing.

Outside, I could hear the voices of the police officers, techs, and everybody else who'd arrived on the scene and were going about their official duties. I was glad I wasn't out there—and not just because Nick was in here.

He stepped closer to me and frowned. "What are you doing here?"

"I came by to pick up some appraisal reports—"

I pressed my lips together. Was it a good idea to tell a homicide detective—even one who lusted after me—that I'd come to the office for the sole purpose of talking to the guy who'd ended up dead?

This seemed like a good time to change the direction of the conversation.

I gestured to Janine and told Nick her name.

"She's the asset manager here," I added. "She saw it happen."

Nick kept frowning at me.

"I come by all the time," I said.

Nick turned up the amperage on his frown.

"It's not unusual," I said, and could hear my voice shake a little.

Nick had a way of getting me rattled. If he frowned

at me for another few seconds, I just might confess to running down Jerry myself.

A few more grueling seconds dragged by and Nick finally took a seat across the table from Janine. He pulled a little notebook from his inside jacket pocket, introduced himself, and gave her his handkerchief.

I didn't know Janine all that well. I'd spoken with her over the phone occasionally and visited here in her office when I'd come to pick up appraisals. Her car had broken down a few weeks ago and I'd given her a ride to work for several days.

I put her age in the mid-twenties range. She was shorter than me—most women are, since I'm five-nine—and had short dark hair. If she hadn't just witnessed a man getting run over by a car and been plummeted into the depth of hysteria, I'd say she was a little frumpy. But in view of the circumstances, I'll be generous and call her curvy.

"Can you tell me what happened?" Nick asked. "Did you see anything unusual when you pulled in?"

Janine wiped her nose and gulped a few times. "Well, Dana was here. I saw her car."

Nick threw me another frown, and then turned back to Janine.

She gulped and another wave of tears washed down her cheeks.

"The next thing I saw was Jerry coming out of the back door of the insurance office," Janine said. "He was bringing the appraisals to our office. He always does that when he knows Dana's coming by to pick them up."

Nick threw another frown at me.

"Then a car just came out of nowhere," she said and sniffed hard. "And it hit him."

———

"Did you recognize the car?" Nick asked.

"It was like Dana's car," she said.

Nick hit me with a frown that morphed into something darker.

"I didn't see who was driving!" Janine suddenly sat straight up in her chair. "I swear, I don't know who it was! I have no idea!"

"What the hell is going on here?" Came a voice from the doorway.

Eric Hunter, the branch manager, strode into the break room scowling at everyone. Nick got to his feet and introduced himself.

A lot of women thought Eric Hunter was good looking. I was one of them. There was a smooth, sophisticated ease about him. He'd just turned thirty. I knew this because I'd attended an after-work birthday celebration for him at a nearby restaurant last week. Eric had light brown hair, blue eyes, and a wife, whom I'd met at the birthday celebration, who was both beautiful and had exquisite taste in men's clothing, judging from how well Eric always dressed.

He'd taken over the helm of the Bonita branch about six months ago, even though he was young for the job. But he'd proved his worth. Almost immediately, the branch had skyrocketed to the enviable position of top profit producer in our division. Every month his branch posted incredible gains. Eric Hunter was the golden boy of Mid-America Financial Services, and he made it look easy.

But he didn't look so smooth at the moment. Right now, he looked mad.

"I just got here," Eric said, nodding toward the rear parking lot. "The place is crawling with cops and nobody will tell me a damn thing."

"A man was struck by a hit-and-run driver," Nick told him. "Jerry Donavan."

"Donavan?" Eric reeled back, and for an instant I thought he was too stunned to speak. He proved me wrong. "Donavan? Damnit!"

"I don't know who did it!" Janine wailed. "I didn't see anything!"

Eric paced a few steps across the break room mumbling a string of curses, then swung around. He popped open the button on his suit coat and planted his hands on his hips, glaring down at Janine. Her sobs ratcheted up, growing higher and louder. Soon, only dogs would be able to hear her.

Or so I hoped.

"I'll get one of the paramedics," Nick said.

No way was I going to be stranded in this tiny room with screaming Janine any longer.

"I'll do it," I shouted, and broke for the door.

Nick, obviously thinking the same, nearly wedged himself in the doorway with me but we both made it through. I glanced back into the break room. Eric continued to glare at Janine.

He looked like he wanted to slap her too.

I lost my nerve at the back door and let Nick go outside to get one of the paramedics. I didn't want to look at Jerry again, or what was left of him.

At the front of the office Gloria stood with the branch's only other employee, Misty. I hadn't seen Misty come into the office but that was probably because I was busy with Janine.

Misty's job at Mid-America was that of cashier. She took payments from walk-in customers, handled the bank deposits, prepared loan documents, and took care of other

---

12

general office duties. She was a recent hire, nineteen years old—and unable to drink at Eric's birthday celebration—a high school graduate who'd opted for work over college. Her clothing and hairstyle screamed senior year.

So there I stood faced with three options: go outside where a dead body waited; return to screaming Janine in the break room; or make small talk with two people I didn't really know or particularly like.

I really had a fourth option, but what does it say about life when the most appealing thing to choose from was to go to work?

I glanced around. No one was watching me. No one had said I couldn't leave. So I left.

I darted in and out of the break room before Eric could saddle me with Janine, snatched my handbag off of the counter, and made my escape.

Using my superhero-like powers of focus and concentration, I kept my gaze on the pavement in front of me and made it to my car without looking at the cops huddled at the crime scene. I drove away without a backwards look.

**

I pulled my Honda into the lot beside Mid-America's branch on Fifth Street, the place I called home for forty-plus hours each week. The office was located in downtown Santa Flores on the ground floor of a two-story building. Just down the block were the post office, the courthouse, and all sorts of restaurants, bars, and office buildings.

There's something comforting about your place of employment. It's familiar. It's secure. You can sit at your desk amid your things and feel accepted, knowledgeable and competent. You have direction, goals, purpose.

Everything else was put aside for those eight hours while you focused on handling the problems put before you, all for the sole gain of the faceless company's bottom line.

I'd worked all sorts of jobs in the past few years, everything from administrative assistant to piercing ears at the mall. The one really good job I'd had was with a major corporation but it went under, dragging me down with it.

So I'd taken the job of asset manager for Mid-America not long ago. The position required that I telephoned customers who were behind on their payments and work with them to get their account up to date. I was okay with helping people get back on their financial feet, especially since I'd experienced some of those problems first hand growing up in a working class family. I'd been trying to manage my own finances, too, in a difficult economy.

It helped that I worked in my hometown. Santa Flores was blessed with a great location halfway between Los Angeles and Palm Springs, at the foot of the mountains leading up to some of the country's best ski resorts. Unfortunately, not much of the good mojo from those fabulous places had rubbed off on Santa Flores. Most of the major industry had moved out years ago, leaving unemployment, gangs, violence, and crime in its place.

I'd lived here for as long as I could remember. My folks lived here, I'd gone to school here, I knew the people here. I understood them. I fit right in.

Mid-America expected me to take whatever steps were necessary to collect their accounts, including pursuing legal action and repossessing collateral. No way was I doing that, so I put my own spin on the position.

I was nice to people. When they ran into financial

trouble and couldn't make their payments, I sometimes fudged a bit on Mid-America's policy. I dished out good karma, allowing my customers to slide a little on our payment, giving them as much wiggle room as I could—as long as my supervisor didn't catch on.

But I liked that about the job. It gave me a chance to be judge, jury, and executioner, at times, to mete out a little justice for my customer's benefit and, occasionally when I was completely out of options, for Mid-America's benefit.

For me, life was all about spreading a little good luck whenever possible.

As I crossed the parking lot and went into the office, I was more than ready to ease into my daily routine and leave murder, mayhem, and manic Janine behind.

That was not to be.

Carmen Hernandez, our cashier who worked at the front counter, leaped to her feet when I walked in.

"Is it true?" she asked, her big brown eyes growing wilder and darker.

Carmen was a few years younger than me but she was already married with children. She looked great, with a fabulous figure and long, dark hair.

The only thing that spread faster than bad news was terrible news. Someone from the Bonita branch, probably Misty, must have called Carmen with a heads-up on what happened to Jerry Donavan.

"Jerry was hit by a car in the alley behind the Bonita branch," I said.

"Is he going to be okay?" Carmen asked.

"No. He's … dead," I said, and headed toward my desk at the back of the office.

Manny Franco, my slightly overweight, severely

stressed-out supervisor, occupied the desk near mine. He was a great boss. If he ever quit Mid-America, I might have to leave too.

Manny was on the phone when I walked past. He gave me an eyebrow bob, which I'd learned long ago meant that we'd talk in a minute.

Inez Marshall, the office manager and Mid-America's version of the Crypt Keeper, wasn't as subtle. She followed me to my desk.

I was usually pretty good at ignoring Inez. I'd been practicing hard at it. As our office manager—just one rung on the corporate ladder below our branch manager, Mr. Burrows, whom we almost never saw—Inez handled the lending side of the business and supervised our two financial reps.

Since, from the look of her, she'd worked for Mid-America since shortly after that huge meteor wiped out the dinosaurs, she'd also put herself in charge of the routine aspects of office life—supplies, timesheets, inter-office memos, meetings. Inez managed to bring new depth to the phrase "daily grind."

Never married and with no children, Inez's entire life was Mid-America. Most of us wished she got out a little more often, preferably on company time, and do something fun, such as clothes shopping.

Inez was still mixing and matching Labor Day's orange/yellow/brown wardrobe pieces, with no chance of anything different until Christmas, when she rounded out her three annual clothes-buying trips.

"Now, Dana," Inez said, taking off her glasses and letting them dangle from the chain around her neck. "I've already called Corporate about what happened this morning."

"I'm doing just fine, Inez," I said, as I dropped my handbag in the bottom drawer of my desk. "Thanks for asking."

"You'll have to talk to legal," Inez said, then lowered her voice. "Now, Dana, there's a certain decorum that must be maintained when talking with our legal department. You'll want to—"

"Maybe you could put it in a memo so I can refer to it often," I said.

"Excellent idea." Inez pursed her lips thoughtfully. "I'll ask Mr. Burrows what to do about your timesheet for this morning."

"That's great, Inez," I called as she trotted back to her desk. "That's exactly what's on my mind right now."

Manny hung up the phone and gave me his come-here head tilt. I settled into the empty chair beside his desk. Carmen joined us.

The other branch employees didn't, but I wasn't surprised.

Jade Crosby, mid-thirties, divorced, mother of two neglected children and one of Mid-America's financial reps, didn't care about anything that didn't directly involve—or benefit—her.

Our other financial rep had resigned so Dennis Bowman had been hired, which meant that a village somewhere was missing its idiot.

Dennis was a little taller and a little older than me, with limp brown hair and glasses that always slid down his nose. He was probably really smart, so smart that he couldn't seem to function in this universe with the rest of us.

I gave Manny and Carmen the rundown. They looked solemn and clucked sympathetically for a few minutes, then Carmen returned to her desk at the front of the office.

"That's rough, real rough," Manny said. "And Janine saw the whole thing?"

"She wasn't handling it well," I said.

"Now, Dana," Inez called, hurrying to join us. "What have you done with the appraisal reports you got from Jerry?"

"They're in police custody," I said. I'd seen them fluttering in the breeze near Jerry's body and knew they'd been taken as evidence.

"You'll need to get them back right away," Inez said.

"I can't get them back."

"I have customers waiting," she said. "I can't process their home equity loans without the appraisal reports."

"Don't you ever watch *Law & Order* re-runs?" I asked.

"Dana, you're going to have to figure out something right away," Inez said. "Our branch is expected to book our required number of loans this month. We can't do that without those appraisals. Corporate is expecting us to meet our monthly goals."

She walked back to her desk.

"How did this get to be my problem?" I asked Manny.

He just shrugged.

"I'll get duplicates," I said.

I went to my desk, anxious to put the disturbing morning behind me. I logged onto my computer and pulled up my collection route, ready to begin calling my customers who were behind on their payments.

Nothing like hearing about someone else's problems

to take your mind off of your own troubles.

I'd made it about halfway through my list of calls when I saw Jade's long blonde hair start to swing from shoulder to shoulder. She did that whenever a good looking man came within fifty feet.

I looked up, never one to ignore the sight of an attractive man, and a thousand little tingles ran up my spine.

Nick Travis stood at the front of the office. He didn't approach the counter, didn't speak. He just waited. I knew what he wanted.

Me.

I walked to the front of the office. As I approached Nick, warmth washed over me, as if he gave off some sort of magnetic beam, drawing me closer.

I made myself stop a few feet from him. He had on his cop face. Not good.

"Solved the crime already?" I asked. "Wow, that's great."

He ignored that.

"You left the scene of a murder," he said.

My stomach rolled but I pushed up my chin and said, "Yeah? So?"

"So Donavan was coming to meet you this morning," Nick said. "He was in the alley where he was killed because of you."

I gulped but kept my chin up. "Yeah? So?"

"So your car was identified by the only eyewitness to the crime," he said.

"Are you going somewhere with this?" I asked.

Nick leaned in a little.

"I'm here to interview the prime suspect," he said. "You."

Dorothy Howell

Chapter 3

So much for good mojo.

Barely past ten o'clock on a Monday morning and here I was the prime suspect in a murder investigation.

Nick pushed open the office door. I stood there and let him hold it for a few seconds, then walked outside. The sky was still overcast but it wasn't cold—it's seldom cold in Santa Flores. We might have a lot of murders, but our weather was great.

Nick led the way around the corner of the building to the parking lot.

"Why did you leave the crime scene?" he asked, his cop face still firmly in place.

"What makes you so sure it was a murder?" I asked. "I mean, how do you know it wasn't an accident? Maybe the driver was too scared to stop? Or blinded by the morning sun? Or distracted, or something?"

"Why did you leave the scene?" Nick repeated.

I guess I hadn't done such a hot job of throwing him off. I tried again.

"You're trying to say that makes me look guilty?" I asked.

"No, you're managing to look guilty all on your own."

"I can't believe you'd attach one ounce of credibility to what Janine Ferris told you," I said. "She was hysterical."

Which was also the way I was starting to sound, I

realized.

I drew in a breath to calm myself.

"Look, Nick, Jerry could have been in that alley for reasons other than coming to see me. Maybe he was meeting someone else? Or going to the deli? Or having a smoke?" I said. "And, yeah, whoever ran him down might have been driving a car similar to mine. It's a black Honda Civic. There must be a million of them on the road."

"A million, huh? That's your alibi?"

The great thing about relationships was the subtle nuances involved. Not that I'm great at anything subtle, but I had this one figured out.

When you got to know someone you discovered all sorts of little tells that gave them away. A crooked grin. Tightly pressed lips. A quirked eyebrow. All the silent cues that spoke volumes.

Nick had his. I'd learned a few of them and saw one now. That little twitch in his left cheek that told me he was just messing with me.

I think Nick liked to yank me around, sometimes, in the hope that I'd offer to have sex with him to get myself out of trouble.

Not a bad idea.

Yet not necessary, at the moment.

"If I'm your best suspect, Sherlock, you're in trouble," I said.

Nick leaned a little closer and his killer smile appeared.

"Maybe I like being in trouble," he said.

Oh, boy. I was the one headed for trouble here. There was no real defense against the Nick Travis smile. It sapped the strength, neutralized vital brain cells, and wiped out the willpower of any female on the receiving end. I felt myself giving in.   Nick   looked   away, releasing me from his sexual tractor beam, and backed up a little. He knew what he was doing.

I did too. And I'd already been messed with enough today.

"Look, Nick, some of us have real jobs," I told him. "I need to get back inside."

"Tell me about Jerry Donavan," he said.

I should do just that. I'd witnessed a murder— almost—and I knew the victim. It was my duty as a citizen to cooperate with law enforcement.

But I wasn't in the mood to cooperate with Nick Travis.

"You first," I said.

I gave him my now-I'm-just-being-stubborn eyebrow lift.

I guess Nick recognized that little tell—he'd seen it a number of times before—because he didn't hesitate but a few seconds before answering.

"It wasn't an accident," he said. "No evidence of an attempt to brake or avoid the victim. The only tire marks were at the entrance of the alley. The driver gunned the engine, hit Donavan at high speed."

Yuck. Now I wished I hadn't asked.

But since I'd started this, I pushed on.

"Any witnesses, other than Janine?" I asked.

"An employee at the deli saw a car—probably the suspect vehicle—speed through the alley. Black, no make or model, no plate number," Nick said.

"I guess I am your best suspect, after all."

Nick shrugged. "Tell me what you know about Donavan."

Each of Mid-America's thousand nationwide

branches made real estate equity loans to customers. A vital part of the process was the property appraisal, so the company had a list of approved appraisers who covered nearly every city, town, and community in the country. Jerry Donavan had been on Mid-America's list for the Santa Flores area for a while. I explained that to Nick.

"Since I live nearby, I always stop to pick up the appraisal reports when he finishes them," I said. "Mid-America is hot to get the loans on the books, so it saves time if I pick them up."

"Did you get to know him?" Nick asked.

I'd hung out with Jerry at a somewhat seedy bar a couple of times, but that was strictly in my official capacity as asset manager for Mid-America. I didn't see any reason to explain that to Nick.

"Jerry rented a space in the back of the insurance office in the same strip mall as the Bonita branch," I said. "The manager of the insurance office was weird about having anybody but Jerry and his assistant in there, so I met him in the Bonita branch."

"He had an assistant?" Nick asked.

"Marsha. She's a real nice lady. She came in a couple of days a week to do office work," I said. "Does she know about Jerry?"

"Nobody's been notified yet," Nick said.

"Donavan always knew ahead of time when you were coming?"

"He, or Marsha, would call to let me know the appraisal reports were finished," I said. "Jerry called last Friday, so I stopped by this morning to pick them up."

"Who else knew you two were meeting there?" Nick asked.

I thought for a few seconds. "Maybe Marsha knew.

I told Manny I'd be late this morning. Everybody in the Bonita branch, probably."

Even though the Bonita branch was part of the same company as the Santa Flores branch and I knew everyone who worked there, going to their office was sort of like visiting a distant cousin's house. You didn't just show up unannounced.

Nick was quiet for a minute or so. "Who would want to kill Jerry Donavan? Any ideas?"

"Take your pick," I said. "He was married three times, that I know of. His ex's are after him for back alimony and child support. There're problems with his kids, his relatives, his friends. He has a drinking problem."

"Sounds as if you knew Donavan well," Nick said.

And it sounded to me as if Nick was trying to make me look guilty.

"Not that well," I insisted.

Nick gave me cop stink-eye.

"He was a talker," I said.

"So him getting run down in an alley doesn't surprise you?" Nick asked.

I hoped I'd never be not-surprised by someone being murdered. Routine stuff for a homicide detective like Nick. But me? Never.

"There was something likeable about the guy," I said. "Besides, none of that stuff was so bad that he deserved to get run over in an alley."

"As far as you know," Nick said.

A little jolt went through me. Nick was right. As far as I knew, Jerry didn't deserve to die like that. But what else was there about Jerry that I didn't know?

Nick seemed to read my thoughts.

"Stay out of this," he told me.

I tried for my innocent look but that one hadn't worked for me in a while. It wasn't working for me now.

"I don't want you poking around in this investigation," Nick said.

"I have to get back to work," I said and headed across the parking lot.

"Dana," Nick said, walking alongside me. "I don't want you involved in this."

I stopped near the office door and glared up at him.

"But you do want me to give you any information I might learn, right?" I asked. "Office gossip? Rumors?"

"I'm always anxious for your cooperation." Nick gave me his little grin. "Your full cooperation."

My heart did a little flip-flop. I hadn't given my *full cooperation* to Nick when he'd been at my apartment a few weeks ago, but I'd come close. Still, the image pinged around in my head.

The office door opened and Carmen leaned out.

"You have a phone call," she said, then giggled. "It's Ronald."

"Who?"

"Your boyfriend, silly," Carmen said, then disappeared inside again.

With supreme effort I managed not to cringe at the mention of Ronald Ashberry's name. Instead, I used this moment to my full advantage.

I straightened my shoulders and looked up at Nick.

"I have to go," I said. "My boyfriend is on the phone. Ronald. He's my boyfriend."

Nick looked unimpressed, as if I'd found myself a boyfriend simply to spite him.

I had, sort of, but for an important reason.

26

"Don't keep him waiting because of me," Nick said.

"I won't," I told him, but didn't move from the spot.

A full minute crept past with me staring up at Nick and him staring back to me. I couldn't seem to break the spell.

"Have dinner with me tonight," Nick said.

"Sure—no!"

I wasn't going to get romantically involved with Nick, and he knew why. He also knew what it would take for me to change my position on us dating, and he'd made it clear he wasn't going to do that.

"I have to go talk to my boyfriend now," I informed him, then put my nose in the air and sailed into the office.

Inside the door, I couldn't help myself—and I hated myself for it—but I looked back. Nick stood at the door watching me. He gave me a half-grin and walked away—which suited me just fine, I told myself as I forced down the butterflies in my stomach and went back to my desk.

Only one phone line was blinking and I figured it was Ronald, dutifully holding for me. Ronald and I had been seeing each other for a couple of weeks now, though it seemed much longer. We weren't official boyfriend-girlfriend. We were simply dating.

Ronald was early-thirties, good looking, never married, no kids, college educated, and employed in a lucrative field. On paper, he was the perfect boyfriend. Most people would wonder why a catch like Ronald was running around unattached.

The reason: he was an engineer and a sports fanatic. The dull and boring double whammy.

All he talked about was his job and sports. He'd told me several times what sort of engineer he was, but I'd never understood what he was talking about. All I knew was that he didn't have anything to do with trains.

Ronald loved sports, every kind of sport. He had teams, players' names, scores and statistics committed to memory stretching back to the original Olympics in Greece, I'm sure, and freely shared that information with anyone who had ears.

So, you might wonder why I'd gotten myself into a relationship with this person, why I'd stayed, and why I was trying so hard to make it work.

Two reasons.

The first was Nick. In my continuing determination to thwart romantic overtures from the one man who refused to do as I wished and divulge information about his high school relationship with my then-best friend, I'd made myself totally unavailable by acquiring a boyfriend.

The other reason was considerably less complicated.

Thanksgiving was almost here, which meant that I was staring down the barrel of the single person's Bermuda Triangle of holidays: Christmas, New Years and Valentine's Day. Ronald, for all his faults, was good looking, and I intended to walk into every upcoming holiday party on the arm of an attractive man.

I can be shallow when the situation warrants.

I picked up the receiver and punched the phone line. I'd asked him to leave a message on my cell phone or send a text message but he refused to do so. He claimed he enjoyed hearing the sound of my voice.

"Good morning," he said. "How are you?"

"It's a madhouse in here," I replied, shuffling papers, trying to make busy noises.

Ronald took several long seconds to digest this.

Ronald took several long seconds to digest everything.

"I thought we should set up something for Thursday," he finally said.

This took me aback. Thursday wasn't a traditional date night, so I shouldn't be expected to hang out with him until the weekend. I was winding up to explain that—in a nice way, of course—when he spoke again.

"Thursday is our special night, after all," he said.

I froze. Our special night? We had a special night? I didn't remember anything special about any night with Ronald.

Frantically I flipped my desk calendar ahead, scanning the notations I'd written. Appointments with clients, accounts to follow up on, my friend Jillian's birthday. But nothing about Ronald.

"Ah, yeah, Thursday," I said. "Wow, is it that time already?

"Two weeks exactly since our first date," Ronald told me.

He remembered that stuff? Good grief.

"I'll pick you up at your place at seven," Ronald said.

Before I could think of a good excuse to get out of it, he said goodbye and hung up. I dropped the phone in the cradle a little annoyed with Ronald, with myself—and with Nick, for some reason—then went back to work.

Nick stayed in my head. He'd asked me if I was surprised that Jerry had been run down in the alley. Then Janine popped into my thoughts and I remembered her screaming, asking who would deliberately do something like that.

The notion intrigued me. Obviously, there was something more about Jerry I didn't know, something so horrible that he'd been killed for it.

What could it be?

Chapter 4

I managed to get through the rest of the day, despite that feeling of heaviness that always hung over me after something awful happened. I wasn't sure if Jerry Donavan's death had brought it on, or my upcoming special night with Ronald.

I decided that a visit to my mom and dad's place was in order, something that would surely lift my flagging spirits.

I drove to their house in an older tract in the Bonita foothills, the home where I grew up along with my brother who was now married and living up north. My parents were the greatest in the world, the Mount Rushmore of parents. I could always count on them to be solid and steady. And tonight, I needed solid and steady.

Nick floated into my mind as I drove and, with some effort, I forced him away. Ronald came next and, with absolutely no effort, I forced him away too.

That left me with Jerry Donavan. Janine Ferris's screams echoed in my head. Why would anyone want to kill him? she'd wailed.

I had no idea.

I parked at the curb outside my parents' house and let myself in with my key.

"Mom? Dad?" I called.

There was always something calming about coming here. The sameness, I guess. Same furniture, same pictures on the walls, everything always in the same place.

No surprises.

I usually got a gleeful call in return, but tonight the house was quiet. In the kitchen, I found Mom standing at the counter, staring down at a cookbook and a tablet.

In her fifties, Mom was tall like me, and had her hair colored every month by her hairdresser. Although none of us remembered her original hair color, she looked great.

But tonight, she looked troubled too. I realized then that she hadn't returned my phone call from yesterday. Very unlike her.

"Mom?" I called, dropping my handbag on the counter.

She looked up, as if I'd startled her.

"Oh, Dana. Hi, honey," she said, and gave me a little hug.

"What are you doing?" I asked.

"Just thinking about my Thanksgiving dinner theme," she said.

My mom couldn't cook a meal or plan a holiday without a theme. She'd done Crock Pot Week, Appetizer Night, Salute to the American Diner, the Fast Food Frenzy, things like that. Christmas last year was themed Christmas in Italy, or as I liked to think of it, the Festival of Carbs.

I guess she wasn't having much luck coming up with this year's Thanksgiving dinner theme because the tablet in front of her was blank. That was totally unlike my mother.

"Where's Dad?" I asked.

The garage door had been closed when I drove up so I knew he wasn't tinkering at his work bench, and I couldn't hear the television playing in the family room—two of my dad's favorite pastimes. I hoped he'd gone to the store for ice cream. Always a favorite and no theme required.

Tears suddenly sprang up in Mom's eyes, causing my heart to spring up into my throat. A thousand thoughts—all of them involving death and serious illness—flashed through my mind.

"What's wrong?" I demanded.

"Your dad is ... he's ..."

"He's what?" I managed not to scream the words.

"He's having an ... affair."

"What?"

Tears rolled down Mom's cheeks. She seemed to age right before my eyes, the heartache, and anguish shrinking her, wrinkling her, devastating her.

"It's true," she said. "I found out by accident."

"What? How? Tell me," I said.

She sniffed, pulled a crumpled tissue from the pocket of her apron and wiped her nose.

"He told me he was helping his friend fix his car. Leo. You remember Leo? The antique car buff? Your dad's been going over to Leo's house night after night, staying for hours," she said, and gulped down another wave of tears. "Two nights ago I needed some milk so I called him. He didn't answer his cell phone, so I called the house. Mildred answered. You remember Mildred? Leo's wife? She said he wasn't there. He hadn't been there at all. He's ... he's been lying to me this whole time."

Mom burst into tears and I wanted to cry too. But more than that, I wanted this to be a huge misunderstanding.

"But, Mom, that doesn't mean he's having an affair," I said. "Have you gotten any odd phone calls? Did you find a secret email account Dad's been using?

Something on Facebook?"

She waved away my words. "There's money missing from our savings account."

I felt as if I'd been stabbed in the chest. My Mount Rushmore parents were solid about everything, especially their finances. One of them would never spend their savings without discussing it.

"Oh, Mom ..."

We hugged and she cried, and I fought back tears while the notion of my dad having an affair filled my mind. It couldn't be true. It just couldn't be.

Mom stepped out of our embrace and forced back her tears.

"I want you to find out for me, Dana," she said. "I want you to follow your dad, see where he goes, who he's ... with."

"No, Mom. I don't want to do that."

"Please, Dana." The tears started again. "I have to know the truth. I can't bear staying in this house night after night, wondering where he is and what he's doing. I need to know for sure. Please, Dana, please do this for me."

Jerry Donavan popped into my mind. Investigating a murder suddenly seemed far less complicated and much more welcome.

***

My dad was having an affair? I couldn't believe it.

The idea raged in my head as I drove away from my parents' house heading to my apartment.

There had to be some simple, logical reason Dad had secretly taken money out of their savings account, lied to Mom about his whereabouts, and spent night after night away from the house. But, honestly, I couldn't imagine what it would be.

Lying in wait for my dad to leave home, then tailing him, spying on him, reporting back to Mom wasn't something I wanted to do. I didn't want to see where he went, who he met, what they did—if, in fact, the whole thing was true. And I sure as heck didn't want to be the one to deliver the devastating news to my mom.

Still, the idea of my dad cheating made me mad. Betraying someone you loved, had spent years with, shared life's ups and downs with, was the worst, as far as I was concerned. If Dad was really up to something, I wasn't sure how I'd react when I learned about it.

I turned onto State Street, silently fuming, imaging how everything about our family would change if this were true. I didn't like the mental picture.

And I didn't like not knowing the truth.

I could only imagine how Mom must feel, not knowing.

I turned at the corner, whipped into my apartment complex and pulled into a parking space. For a few minutes I just sat there, thinking.

No two ways about it, I was going to have to follow my dad and see if he was cheating on my mom.

I dragged myself out of my car, glad that today was almost over and things couldn't get any worse.

And then they did.

Nick Travis stood on the sidewalk outside my building.

My heart did its usual little pitter-patter at the sight of him. He looked especially appealing tonight, with his collar open, his tie pulled down, his hair a little mussed. Not at all intimidating—at least, not in a law enforcement sort of way.

Nick met me as I crossed the parking lot. The

security lighting at my apartment complex was awesome so he looked even better up close.

"Hungry?" he asked, and held up a take-out bag. "Chinese."

Delicious scents wafted from the bag, reminding me that I hadn't eaten dinner and that I was starving. The peanut butter sandwich on week-old bread and last night's reheated mac and cheese that awaited me in my kitchen seemed positively inedible right now.

How did Nick know? How did he always know when to show up, what to bring, how to make my life a little better?

If I wasn't so hungry I might have been really irked.

Nick pulled the bag away. "Unless, of course, I'm interrupting your evening with your new boyfriend."

Nick could be such a dog sometimes. He was a police detective, so I was confident he'd scanned every car in the parking lot when he'd arrived and determined that there wasn't a new vehicle here—he'd been to my place enough times to know, plus it was one of the things that made him a good cop.

Of course, Ronald wasn't upstairs in my apartment waiting for me, nor was he coming by later tonight. In fact, if I'd seen his car when I pulled up, I might have kept driving.

A little pang of guilt hit me. I really needed to re-think my involvement with Ronald.

But there was no way I was going to admit that to Nick.

"He's coming by later," I told him, and glanced at my watch. "I can give you thirty minutes."

Nick leaned in. Warmth rolled off of him, and his masculine scent washed over me, freezing me in place.

"Thirty minutes?" he whispered. "I'll just be getting started after thirty minutes."

Breath went out of me. My knees weakened. A little moan rattled in my throat.

We stood like that, close, our breath mingling, with me caught in Nick's gaze like a helpless butterfly in a sticky web.

Why was I refusing to date Nick? Why was I so determined to keep him at a distance?

Should I rethink that, too?

Nick eased closer and rattled the take-out bag.

"I got extra fortune cookies," Nick said. "Want to predict how our evening will end?"

I started to melt. How could I not?

Then, one stalwart brain cell fired somewhere in the depth of my brain, reminding me of everything and bringing me back to reality.

I stepped back. Cool air swirled between us.

"It will end with Ronald and me having a lovely evening, after you leave," I said. I cut around him, heading for my apartment building, then called, "Hurry up, will you? I'm starving."

I dashed up the exterior staircase to my apartment on the second floor. By the time I reached the landing, Nick was behind me. I unlocked the door and we went inside.

My apartment was terrific, a two-bedroom with a nice-sized living room and a kitchen big enough for a dinette set. I'd struggled to make rent during the months I'd been unemployed or forced to take whatever job I could get. I'd managed to hang on, and I was glad I had.

A little mewling sound came from the kitchen when I switched on the light. Seven Eleven, my sweet little kitty and the world's best roommate, appeared, yawning and stretching. She meowed, rushed past me, and wound her furry body around Nick's ankles.

"Traitor," I mumbled.

"Go change," Nick said, and headed into the kitchen.

It might have annoyed me that he was so at ease in my apartment, but I was hungry and too worn out to mention it.

In my bedroom I undressed, and because it felt odd standing in my underwear when Nick was just steps away, I threw on sweat pants and a T-shirt, then pulled my hair back in a ponytail. When I came down the hallway I saw Nick's sport coat and his shoulder holster hanging on the back of one of my dinette chairs. He'd opened a can of food for Seven Eleven and she was lapping it up.

He'd set the take-out on my living room coffee table, gotten two beers from my fridge, and tuned my television to a basketball game. We filled our plates and settled at opposite ends of my sofa.

A few minutes passed with Nick watching the game and me watching him while we ate. The food was good and so was the beer. I started to relax.

Relaxing at home with Nick felt nice.

We finished eating and took the leftovers and our plates into the kitchen. Nick got another beer from the fridge and passed it to me. I hesitated, but took it. He got one for himself and we went back into the living room.

"What's going on in the Bonita branch?" Nick asked, and switched off the television.

I had the beer bottle almost to my lips, but stopped and said, "Is this some sort of investigative technique? Get a suspect liquored up and question them?"

"Depends on the suspect," Nick said. "What's

going on in that office?"

I took this to mean that Nick was short on suspects in Jerry Donavan's murder and was fishing for some useful information.   I felt, too, that the personnel in Mid-America's Bonita branch was a good place to start, given that everyone there had known Jerry was meeting me this morning.

"The office is doing great," I said. "After Eric took over, it shot up in the standings and has been our district's highest profit earner, and one of the biggest company-wide. Eric is a Mid-America golden boy."

Nick nodded and tipped up his beer.

"Any leads?" I asked, before he could ask me another question.

He took his time swallowing the beer, then shook his head.

"How about surveillance tape?" I asked.

"Nothing at the strip mall," he said.

Leave it to Corporate to locate the office in a questionable neighborhood, then not make sure there was adequate security.

"We got something from an office building across the street and down the block. It's a side angle. No license plates visible. Too grainy to see a driver. But lots of small black cars, like the suspect vehicle," Nick said. "What about the other people who work in the branch?"

Even though all Mid-America employees were assigned to a specific branch, we often talked to each other on the phone, got acquainted at company meetings, and visited other branches occasionally. We got to know each other. And, of course, like every other company, there was always gossip. If something went down in one of the branch offices, the phone lines lit up.

"Gloria Colton is the assistant manager. She's been around forever, worked in a lot of different branches, but never got promoted past her position. I don't know why. And Misty? She was hired just a month or so ago. She graduated from Eastside last spring."

Nick froze mid-swallow and cut his eyes to me at the mention of Eastside, the high school we'd both attended. We'd been there together for only one year—that fateful year with Katie Jo.

"Eric Hunter went to Eastside," Nick said.

"You're kidding," I said. "I had no idea."

"He was a year ahead of me," Nick said. "He graduated before you got there."

My thoughts rushed back a decade and I realized that Eric had been in the same graduating class as my older brother Rob. I wondered if they'd known each other.

Then I realized something else. When I'd gone to the after-work birthday celebration for Eric, he'd claimed he was turning thirty, which didn't add up. He must have somehow managed to graduate early—or he'd lied about his age.

"Did you and Eric know each other?" I asked.

"I knew *of* him," Nick said. "We weren't friends."

I didn't ask if Nick had mentioned their high school history to Eric during his investigation at the Bonita branch this morning. Nick would never talk about anything personal under those circumstances.

"Do you think Janine Ferris recognized the driver?" Nick asked.

The question stunned me. I hadn't considered it— which was why Nick was a detective and I wasn't.

"It might explain why she was over-the-top hysterical," he said.

"Why wouldn't she have told you?" I asked.

Nick shrugged. "It happens. Witnesses aren't sure what they actually saw. They don't want to wrongly accuse somebody."

I considered the possibility and replayed the image in my head of Janine standing by her car screaming in horror, then screaming in the break room. Maybe she had seen the driver, or maybe she routinely fell apart in a crisis. I didn't know her well enough to say.

"It's possible," I said.

Nick stewed on that for a few seconds, then shook it off as if it were yet another theory that might—or might not—pan out.

We sat in silence for a few minutes, then Nick looked at his watch.

"Ronald's late," he said.

"Who?"

"Your boyfriend," Nick said, and the corner of his lip turned up in a sly smile.

Maybe I shouldn't have gotten Ronald involved with my quest to keep Nick at arm's length. Maybe I should have just made up an imaginary new boyfriend—at least a pretend-boyfriend wouldn't be annoying or inconvenient or late.

"He probably stopped to pick up ice cream," I said. "He loves to surprise me."

Nick kept giving me that half smile and nodded.

"I'd better get out of here and leave you two love birds to your ice cream," he said, and rose from the sofa.

I followed him into the kitchen. He put on his shoulder holster and sport coat, and I walked with him to the door.

"Thanks for dinner," I said.

41

We stood there looking at each other for a long moment, then Nick left. I closed the door behind him.

"Lock the door, Dana," he called from outside.

I looked out the peep hole as I turned the dead bolt. He waved—that dog, he knew I'd be watching. He headed down the steps.

I'd had a thing for Nick since way back in high school. He was a senior when my best friend Katie Jo Miller and I were sophomores. Nick and Katie Jo had dated. She'd gotten pregnant. He'd made her have an abortion, then dumped her and left town.

At least, that was the rumor. Katie Jo never told me anything about what happened. She'd stopped coming to school, stopped calling me, stopped hanging out. But everybody, including me, knew the rumor was true.

Nick had finally moved back to Santa Flores not long ago and we'd gotten involved during a homicide investigation. Something sparked between us. But I couldn't get past what Nick had done to Katie Jo, and when I'd finally gotten up the nerve to confront him, he'd told me it was none of my business.

Just like that. None of my business.

Technically, he was right. Nothing about the incident involved me, except that Katie Jo had been my best friend. It was years ago. We'd all grown up, become adults, gotten jobs, become responsible citizens—no longer high school kids.

But I couldn't let go of what Nick had done. I'd told him that. He refused to explain what had happened. Flat refused.

High school was a long time ago. So why wouldn't he tell me? Why keep it a big secret? Especially after I'd told him there could never be anything serious going on

---

42

with us as long as that issue was between us.

So here we were drawn to each other, suspended in this weird relationship where he was trying to wear me down and make me let go of something that was extremely important to me. And here I was determined to keep him away until he came clean about the whole thing.

I switched off the lights and headed down the hallway.

Maybe I should let it go.

But if Nick kept something a secret that was this important to me and I let him get by with it, what would that mean for a long-term relationship? Would he always decide what he wanted to tell me and what he didn't? Would I fall into the practice of always letting those things go?

In the bathroom, I got my toothbrush from the medicine cabinet just as Seven Eleven jumped up onto the toilet lid.

"It's just you and me again tonight," I said. "I didn't need a fortune cookie to predict it."

I thought about how the evening might have turned out, then forced the thought from my mind.

This was for the best, I decided.

But was it good fortune?

I wasn't sure.

Chapter 5

"What's wrong with Mom?"

Nothing like a call from an older sibling first thing in the morning—especially one that didn't start with a greeting or a pleasantry, just a demand. But that was my brother Rob. I'd gotten used to it.

When I'd seen his name on my cell phone caller ID, I'd hesitated to answer, and not because I was driving, running a few minutes behind and didn't want to be late for work. I was afraid he'd found out about our mom's suspicion that Dad was having an affair, and it was way too early in the morning to discuss it.

"Why?" I asked, as I swung into the Mid-America parking lot. "What happened?"

"Nothing happened," Rob said, as if that explained everything.

"Something happened," I said, as I whipped into a space and killed the engine. "You wouldn't be calling me otherwise."

Rob had gotten married not long ago and he and his new wife lived up north, so he didn't see the family often.

"Mom hasn't called," he said. "She hasn't emailed. She hasn't texted. Nothing. Two days and I haven't heard from her."

My mom wasn't a nag or an overbearing mother, but she was always concerned about Rob and me. She worried about us, wanted to know if we were okay, if we needed something, if there were problems, if there was anything she could do to help. So with two days gone and no word from her, I could see why Rob was worried.

"She's not sick, if that's what you mean," I said, as I gathered my things and got out of my Honda.

"Then what's wrong?" he asked.

I could tell from Rob's voice that he was genuinely concerned about Mom and I was tempted to tell him what was going on. But I knew he'd call Mom right away, and I wasn't sure that having her repeat the whole upsetting story was a good idea. Of course, finding out that Mom suspected Dad was having an affair would be upsetting for Rob, too. I figured it was better to keep the news to myself until I'd found out exactly what was going on.

"I saw her last night," I said, as I crossed the parking lot. "She was in a semi-panic because she hasn't come up with her Thanksgiving dinner theme yet."

"Oh. Okay," Rob said, and I could hear the relief in his voice.

"Are you and Denise coming down for Thanksgiving?" I asked, anxious to move the conversation to a different topic.

"Sure. If Mom doesn't cancel because she can't come up with a theme," he said, and chuckled. "Are you bringing a date this year?"

Nick flashed in my mind. I pushed him out. Then Ronald appeared in his place. I pushed him out too.

"You just want me to bring a date to distract Mom," I said, "so she won't start asking you and Denise when you're going to give her a grandbaby."

I stopped outside Mid-America's entrance. Traffic was heavy on Fifth Street as everybody hurried to get to work, stirring up a little breeze.

"Want to hear something crazy?" I asked. "I met a

guy you went to high school with. Eric Hunter. Remember him?"

"Oh, yeah. I remember Eric."

"We work for the same company," I said.

"He's not in jail?" Rob asked.

I stepped away from the building and pressed my cell phone closer to my ear.

"Eric was trouble back then?" I asked.

"He had a psycho girlfriend who used to steal CDs from the store where Eric worked," Rob said. "He looked the other way while she pocketed them."

I'd shoplifted a lipstick when I was in high school. Not one of my finer moments, but not exactly a felony either.

"So it was just normal high school stuff?" I asked.

"They sold the CDs at school. Made a fortune." He was quiet for a few seconds. I imagined him sitting at his desk, gazing across the room, remembering his days at Eastside. "That girlfriend of his—what was her name? Nora. No, Nola. Nola Miles. She was a real piece of work. Completely psycho about Eric. It was crazy."

"She was a nut and he still dated her?" I asked.

"Eric was just as psycho about her," Rob said. He paused for another few seconds. "Guess it was just one of those high school things. Glad to hear it turned around for Eric. Listen, Dana, I've got to get to a meeting."

"We'll talk later," I said, and ended the call.

I used my key to open the door—all the employees had a key since we had to work a half hour before and after our official hours of operation—and went inside. Everyone else was already shuffling papers or sipping break room coffee. Mr. Burrows, the branch manager, had the only private office in the place and his door was closed, as usual.

Inez gave me stink-eye as I walked past her desk. She glanced from me to the wall clock, then jotted something on her calendar. I was sure she intended to check my timesheet at the end of the week and make sure I'd noted that I was four minutes late.

Four minutes was no big deal, as I saw it. Being late at all was hardly the crime against humanity that Inez considered it. Yet employers were always harping on the importance of reporting to work on time. Personally, I believed that what I accomplished after I got here was the most important thing

Manny was on the telephone as I passed his desk, already looking stressed and worn out. A tall stack of folders was at his elbow, and his computer monitor was surrounded by yellow sticky notes. He nodded, listening, and waved me over.

"The DM wants you go work in the Bonita branch this afternoon," Manny whispered, covering the receiver. "Janine is going to be out for a while"

"Is the district manager going to cut me some slack when my own work gets behind?" I asked.

"Of course not," Manny said, and turned back to his telephone conversation.

I dropped my handbag in my desk drawer and, as I sat down, Eric Hunter flew into my head. I'd been surprised by what Rob had told me about Eric's high school days. Allowing his girlfriend to steal from the store where he worked, then joining her in selling the stolen items? That was far worse than the lipstick I'd shoplifted. Definitely not a typical high school move.

But Eric had turned things around. Whatever had happened to him after leaving high school had been for the best—probably getting rid of the psycho girlfriend helped. He was a hard worker now, ambitious, anxious to move into Mid-America's upper management, apparently.

So was that the kind of man who arrived late for work? I didn't think so. And was it a coincidence that Eric had been late on the morning of Jerry's murder?

I replayed that morning's events in my head, calculating the timeline as best I could—hearing the roar of a car engine; Janine's screams; rushing into the alley; getting her into the break room; the arrival of the police. All of that had happened before Eric showed up.

A chill swept through me. By my own very unscientific method, it seemed to me that Eric—driving a car that he'd possibly stolen—had time to run Jerry down in the alley, speed away, jump into his own pre-positioned vehicle, and drive back.

Could Eric have killed Jerry?

I thought about how Eric had seemed when he'd arrived that morning. A myriad of emotions ran through my head. Was he stunned? Upset? Shocked? None of those seemed quite right. If anything, Eric had seemed angry. But angry at what?

Of course, there was no motive—not one that I knew of. Plus, Eric hardly seemed the type, even after what Rob had told me about Eric's high school antics. Selling stolen CDs was a long way from committing murder.

"Attention! Attention in the branch!" Inez called from her desk.

"Holy crap," Manny grumbled.

"Our weekly meeting will commence immediately," Inez announced.

"We're having a meeting?" I asked and groaned.

"Didn't you read my memo, Dana?" Inez asked.

I glanced down and saw a memo that Inez had written and distributed this morning. Seven people in our office—counting Inez—and she sent a memo. Good grief.

"Please gather at my desk at this time," Inez called.

Manny and I exchanged a long suffering sigh, dragged ourselves and our chairs to Inez's desk and plopped down. Jade, Dennis, and Carmen did the same.

"We're going to have to cut our meeting short this morning," Inez said, "since Dana was late coming in today."

"Come in late on meeting day from now on," Manny whispered to me.

Inez slid on her glasses and consulted the agenda she'd typed.

"First of all, I want to get an update from each of you on Mid-America's Thanksgiving food drive," Inez said. "How many donations have each of you received?"

Everybody's gaze wandered to the floor, the ceiling, out the door—everywhere but to Inez—mine included.

Mid-America's latest attempt to make itself look good at the expense of us employees was their Thanksgiving food drive. We'd received a memo from Corporate several weeks ago, which Inez had gleefully distributed and diligently followed up on, as per the memo's accompanying instructions.

Each employee was required to contact grocery stores and markets in the neighborhood, present the manager with a Mid-America flier explaining the program, and get food donations. Then, each branch was supposed to tally their results and transport everything to a food bank in Los Angeles for distribution. The office collecting the largest number of items would receive national recognition in the company newsletter and a plaque to display in their break room.

From the expression on everyone's face, neither the write-up in the newsletter nor the plaque had motivated any of us to go out and ask for donations. It certainly hadn't done it for me. After all, Mid-America was a major corporation that made huge profits and could have simply donated cash to the food bank without making the employees do all the legwork.

Inez pulled out another corporate form and picked up a pen.

"Dennis?" she asked. "How much have you collected?"

"Uh, well, nothing yet," he said. "But I'm on it."

"Carmen?" Inez asked.

"Nothing," she said.

"Jade?"

So far my morning was off to a less than stellar start. I was going to need some serious mojo improvement to get through the day.

* * *

After lunch, I shut down my computer, gathered my things and left the office. I also left much of my work undone, but since I'd been directed to help out in the Bonita branch for the afternoon, there was nothing I could do about it.

I got in my car and pulled onto Fifth Street, then turned left onto Fleming Avenue. It would have been quicker to take the freeway that ringed Santa Flores but since I was on company time, I saw no need to rush.

When driving, I usually turned on my favorite music, allowed my mind to wander, and got lost in the solitude. But instead, I kept thinking about my theory that

50

Eric had run down Jerry in the alley, then returned to the office in his own car that he'd left nearby.

Had the police looked for the suspect vehicle in the nearby neighborhood? Should I should call Nick and ask?

The idea floated in my brain for a few minutes, then I disregarded it. Nick had most certainly done a neighborhood search. I was also sure he'd checked out body shops, including those known for their questionable ethics, to see if anyone had tried to get front-end repairs done. True, the vague description of a small black car wasn't much to go on, but probably enough.

I turned onto State Street and drove several blocks to the Bonita office. Parking in the employees' lot behind the strip mall was out of the question—I didn't want to look at the spot where Jerry had been killed—so I swung into the front parking lot and found a space near the deli.

As I got out of the car I heard shouts. In front of the insurance office I spotted two women, a teenage girl, and a man involved in a confrontation, all of them yelling at each other. A police car was positioned nearby and two officers were in the mix.

Had someone else been murdered?

Chapter 6

"Dana!"

A woman separated from the group and hurried toward me. It was Marsha, Jerry's part-time office help. One of the women yelled and tried to follow her, but a police officer stopped her.

"Dana," Marsha cried, rushing to meet me. "Thank goodness you're here. I'm so glad to see a friendly face."

Marsha was easily in her fifties, with a stocky figure and red hair pulled back in a bun. She'd gone white beneath the sprinkling of freckles on her cheeks and nose.

"What the heck is going on?" I asked.

The woman who'd attempted to pursue Marsha was still being held at bay by the police officer. The teenage girl had joined them.

"That's Jerry's ex-wife—one of them, anyway," Marsha said, edging closer to me. "And her daughter."

I saw the resemblance then. Both had blonde hair, though the mom's was over-forty short, and the daughter's was still-in-high-school long.

"I was sitting in the office trying to make heads or tails out of everything Jerry left," Marsha said, "when in stormed Patricia. And she brought Brooke with her. Can you imagine? Bringing your teenage daughter for back-up?"

The police officer was getting an earful from Patricia and Brooke. The other officer was dealing with the man, whom I didn't recognize.

"That's Mr. Perkins, the insurance agent who rents—rented—space to Jerry," Marsha said. "Persnickety old codger. Called the cops."

"What does Patricia want?" I asked, keeping a wary eye on her.

"Money. What else?" Marsha said. "She accused me of holding back Jerry's money, keeping it from her. She says it belongs to her now."

"Doesn't she have to wait until Jerry's will is read?" I asked.

"Jerry was behind on his alimony and child support. He was always behind. I know it's been hard on Patricia. Besides Brooke, she's got two other teenagers at home."

"Was there insurance money?" I asked.

Marsha nodded. "Yes, but you know how long those things take."

The police officer was herding Patricia and Brooke toward their car and it looked as if they were going willingly. Then Brooke turned back.

"This isn't over, Marsha!" she screamed. "My mom's going to get what belongs to her, one way or the other!"

Brooke spun away from the police officer and ran to a car. She jumped in behind the wheel and started the engine as Patricia climbed in on the passenger side. Brooke whipped the car out of the parking space and drove away.

With that, Mr. Perkins marched over. He was sixtyish, with a carefully styled comb-over and a neat mustache, and dressed in a three-piece suit. The two police officers followed.

"I can't have this," he told Marsha. "I'm running a respectable business and I can't, and I won't, have this sort of thing going on. You need to clear out right away."

Mr. Perkins spun around and headed toward his office. The police officers got into their patrol car and drove off.

"Oh, dear," Marsha sighed.

"Do you want to come into our break room for a few minutes and calm down?" I asked.

"If I thought it would help, I'd do it," Marsha said. She shook her head. "I've got a real mess on my hands. The police took most everything out of Jerry's office, including his computer. "

"The appraisal reports," I realized.

Mid-America wasn't Jerry's only client. He did appraisals for many other lending institutions, and the data he'd compiled for each of them was on his computer.

"Without Jerry's finished appraisal report, dozens and dozens of home sales and refinances are going to be delayed," Marsha said.

"We'll have to find a new appraiser," I said. "Everybody's loan will be delayed for weeks."

"Plus, Jerry's won't get paid for the work he did, and I've still got his bills to pay," Marsha said. "I've got a lot of Jerry's stuff backed up on my computer at home. I'll see what I can come up with."

"Thanks, Marsha," I said. "I know this is a tough time for you."

"Tougher for Jerry," she said with a rueful smile. "And darn, wouldn't you know it? Just when he was finally getting his life together, this happened."

This surprised me. "Jerry was getting his life together? How?"

"I didn't ask. I was just grateful."

Marsha headed toward the insurance office and I

walked inside the Mid-America branch.

Misty sat at her usual spot at the front counter and Gloria was at her desk just behind her. An empty desk that had been occupied by Janine was situated nearby. Eric was positioned at the rear of the office.

Not all Mid-America offices had the same number of employees. That was determined by how many accounts were on the books. If an office was growing, acquiring new business, they were entitled to more employees. In the Santa Flores branch where I worked there were seven of us. Here, there were only four—three now that Janine was out—but that was changing. Thanks to Eric's management skills, the branch was growing by leaps and bounds—as was Eric's monthly bonus—and would soon qualify for another employee.

Not that these employees looked like they were having such a great time. Misty gave me a quick smile when I walked past. Gloria glanced up but didn't speak. Eric waved me to his desk.

He was impeccably dressed, as usual, not a hair out of place. Handsome in a way that made women look twice at him.

"I don't know why the DM sent you." Eric frowned and still he looked good. "We don't need help."

That suited me fine. The atmosphere was tense in here. Gloria didn't like me, for some reason, and I had plenty of my own work to do in the Santa Flores branch. Still, it annoyed me that Eric wasn't the least appreciative of my putting all my responsibilities aside and coming to help out.

Eric stewed for another minute, then huffed. "Since you're here you may as well run through Janine's collection route."

I sat down at Janine's desk and logged onto the computer, then tapped a couple of keys and a list of delinquent accounts flashed onto the screen. The computer kept track of all the past due customers according to how late their payments were, thirty, sixty, ninety, or over ninety days.

"Dana?" Eric called. "Janine was handling the Thanksgiving food drive. She must have a list of merchants who pledged donations. Find it and put it on my desk."

I picked up the telephone and started making calls. Customers walked in and Misty took their payments at the front counter. Gloria took loan applications over the phone. Eric went to lunch.

Janine had been doing a good job working the accounts, I could see. Every time a Mid-America employee spoke with a customer we were required to note the conversation in the comments section. Janine had consistently called all the past due accounts and was working with them to get caught up.

I kept dialing for dollars, as the old saying went, getting promises from customers on when they would send their payment, then marking the account accordingly. It was all pretty routine stuff, until the computer presented me with an account accompanied by a tiny red flag. A first payment default.

Any company lending money was always on guard against fraud. Identity theft was a massive problem. So a brand new account that hadn't had one single payment made on it caused alarm bells to go off. No branch manager wanted to admit he'd made a loan to someone who'd out-and-out lied, who'd given fraudulent information, and had taken the loan proceeds with no intention of paying it back.

Still, it could simply mean that the new customer was unaccustomed to the payment date and had forgotten. Hopefully, that would be this Mick Dudley's excuse.

I phoned his home and got a recording saying the number was out of service. Next I tried his place of employment, and was told that I had the wrong number. The guy who answered his cell number had never heard of Mick Dudley.

At this point there was nothing to do but get the original paper application and go over all the information. I went to the file cabinet and pulled out the folder.

"What are you doing?" Gloria demanded.

Startled, I jumped, then saw that she was standing right behind me.

"I'm checking the folder," I told her. "I found a first payment default."

"Eric handles those," Gloria said.

"I've got the file right here," I said. "I can follow up—"

"That's the way Eric wants it done." She pulled the file folder out of my hand. "I'll give it to him when he comes back from lunch."

Gloria went back to her desk, taking the file folder with her.

Of course, the other problem with a first payment default was that someone in the branch might have made the loan to a fictitious person and pocketed the proceeds. That person was usually the manager.

Had Eric done that? Since I already suspected him of murdering Jerry, nothing else was out of the realm of possibility.

I returned to my desk and picked up the telephone but

couldn't bring myself to punch out a number. It occurred to me that I might have found Eric's motive for murdering Jerry. Maybe Eric had made a loan to Jerry, which was strictly forbidden by Mid-America, then gotten cold feet, feared for his job, and killed Jerry to cover it up.

I let the notion play around in my head for a while, then decided that it was thin, very thin. But still worth checking out.

I changed screens on the computer and did a name search for an account held by Jerry Donavan. Nothing popped.

Well, so much for that theory.

I started calling customers again. A few minutes later, a couple walked into the office and inquired about a loan. Misty showed them to one of the interview rooms, and Gloria went in to talk with them.

Another customer came into the office and while Misty was busy taking his payment, I slipped my cell phone out of my handbag and went to Gloria's desk. I opened the Mick Dudley file folder and flipped through the documents. Eric had handled the entire transaction. I took photos of everything, closed the folder and went back to my desk.

Misty's customer left. She darted to my desk.

"Oh my God, so what was going on outside?" Misty whispered. "I saw, like, the cops and everything."

"Jerry's ex-wife," I said.

Misty made a pouty face. "Poor Jerry. I liked him. I used to see him out back and we'd, you know, have a smoke and talk. He was a really nice guy."

Misty had worked here for a short while so she hadn't had time to know the real Jerry.

"Too bad Eric was late for work that day. I mean, he

might have seen who did it," Misty said.

"Eric is usually on time?" I asked.

"Early most of the time. He's kind of, you know, kind of psycho about things," she said, and waved the stack of papers in her hand. "Like this bill. I have to write a check to have the baseboard in the interview room repaired. A customer accidently scuffed it. Eric had somebody come out that same day and fix it. A hundred bucks. I mean, really? A hundred bucks? Can you believe it?"

"He seems to be big on appearances," I said.

"Yeah, I know." Misty blushed. "He's so handsome. Don't you think he's handsome? He could be screwing around on his wife big-time, but he's not."

"How do you know?" I asked.

"They're so much in love," Misty said. "She comes in the office all the time. I can hear him talking to her on the phone, like, all the time. Seriously. All the time."

"Have you heard from Janine?" I asked.

"She's completely lost her mind, you know? But you can't blame her, I guess. She knew Jerry, too. You know, smoke breaks in the alley," Misty said. "Eric said not to bother her. He thinks she's going to sue the company."

"Sue?" I asked. "For what?"

Chairs scraped the floor in the interview room and voices got louder. Misty dashed back to the front counter as Gloria walked out with the couple she'd been talking to about a loan.

I picked up the phone and started calling customers again. My mind wandered while I was on hold and listening to recorded messages.

I'd seen Eric and Lourdes together at the after-work birthday celebration and they were a striking couple. Eric was as handsome as Lourdes was beautiful. That night she'd styled her blonde hair in an elegant up-do and worn expensive on-trend clothing. They seemed to be building a dynasty of sorts, with Eric climbing the Mid-America corporate ladder, and Lourdes managing the vintage shop she'd opened in the quaint, revitalized section of Santa Flores down on Sixth Street.

By all accounts, Eric and Lourdes were desperately in love. I wondered about that girlfriend he'd left behind after high school, the one who'd sold stolen CDs with him.

Maybe everything about high school was meant to be left behind.

Nick flew into my head. Him too?

I let the image of him stay in my thoughts for a while. I had feelings for him, and I was pretty sure he felt something for me. I was refusing to act on them. Was that a mistake?

Poor dead Jerry came into my head next. He and Patricia must have loved each other once. They'd had three kids together. Now Jerry was gone and the neglect and mismanagement of his own life had turned her into something of a raving lunatic, causing a public scene and getting the cops involved.

I felt bad for their daughter Brooke. Apparently, this problem between Jerry and Patricia had gone on for years and become such a big part of daily life that now Brooke had been dragged into it.

Patricia was desperate for money, according to Marsha. Desperate enough to run down Jerry for his insurance money?

The long afternoon finally ended. I shut down the computer.

"I checked Janine's desk," I said to Eric. "I couldn't

find a list of merchants willing to donate to the Thanksgiving food drive."

Eric mumbled under his breath and shook his head in disgust.

I grabbed my handbag. Gloria didn't speak. Misty gave me a little wave as I went out the door.

The evening air was cool and crisp, a welcome relief from the oppressive office atmosphere. I hoped the district manager wouldn't ask me to work there again.

Of course, just because my time at Mid-America was up that didn't mean I was done for the day.

I got in my car and headed for my parents' house.

Chapter 7

Was I different from Brooke Donavan?

The idea came to me as I sat in my car down the block from my parents' house, waiting for my dad to leave. I knew what time Mom always served dinner—though Dad would be lucky to get a grilled cheese sandwich out of her these days—so I figured that being parked with my headlights off, slouched down in the seat wouldn't last long.

Brooke, a pretty girl probably in her senior year, should be spending her time twirling that long hair of hers, talking about some guy she liked, Facebooking and tweeting her friends. Instead, she was in the middle of her parents' bad relationship.

Here I was in the same situation. Only I was more covert about it.

The front door opened and my dad walked out of the house. It was dark but the street lights lit the area well enough for me to see that he was dressed in his usual work pants and shirt. He went to his pickup truck parked at the curb, got in, and pulled away. I waited until I saw his tail lights disappear around the corner, then started my car and followed.

My dad was a nice-looking man. He was in his fifties, tall, still had most of his hair, and was a little thick around the middle from too many of my mom's good meals coupled with Clint Eastwood and John Wayne movie marathons. While it was possible he was having an affair, as Mom suspected, I didn't want to believe it was true—nor did I want to think about it in too much detail.

I hung back and followed him out of our neighborhood, then east on State Street. Dad kept going when the city of Bonita turned into the city of Maywood.

Maywood had been created several years ago when developers had plowed under the massive orange groves that had covered the foothills for a century, and put in huge, expensive homes. Dad's friend Leo, whom he was supposed to be spending his evenings with, didn't live there. None of my parents' friends lived there.

I started to feel kind of sick.

Dad turned right. I fell back a little, then turned in time to see him pull into a driveway halfway down the block. I whipped in behind a BMW parked at the curb three houses up, and killed the engine and my headlights. Dad got out of his truck and walked to the front door. The porch light came on. A woman opened the door. She was expecting him. She smiled. They went inside together.

I wanted to cry.

Mom had been right.

I wanted to throw up.

My dad was having an affair.

Anger, hurt, outrage shot through me. I couldn't believe this was happening. I just couldn't believe it. But I'd seen it with my own eyes. There was no denying it.

How could my dad do this? How could he cheat on my mom? They'd known each other since high school.

And how was I going to tell Mom?

I sat in the dark, my eyes trained on the house. I'd always known my parents' marriage was strong. They'd been together for decades. I never saw them fight and seldom heard them disagree.

Had their time together finally played itself out? Or was it another high school romance that was never meant to be, that should have been left behind after graduation?

Knuckles rapped on my window. I screamed and jumped up, banging my head.

Nick glared in the window at me.

"What are you doing here?" he shouted.

Good grief. How was I supposed to run a covert operation with a homicide detective hanging around my car?

"Get in," I shouted back.

He circled the car and climbed into the passenger seat.

"You nearly gave me a heart attack," I said, and rubbed the top of my head. "And maybe a concussion."

"What are you doing here?" Nick demanded.

I wasn't feeling particularly generous of spirit right now.

"What are *you* doing here?" I shot back.

He huffed. "You know better than to get involved in this."

I gasped. How had Nick found out about my parents' affair?

"How could I *not* get involved?" I demanded.

"Because it doesn't concern you," he said.

"Doesn't *concern* me?" I repeated at the top of my lungs. "Have you *lost your mind?*"

Nick looked at me, paused for a few seconds then said, "We're not talking about the same thing, are we?"

No way was I admitting to anything.

"You first," I said.

Nick shifted in the seat and frowned, then nodded across the street and down the block.

"I was here questioning Eric Hunter," he said.

"Eric?" I sat up straighter in the seat. "Eric lives here?"

I looked at the houses that lined the street. Massive two-story homes with crystal chandeliers visible through vestibule fanlights, paved circular driveways, lush landscaping with fountains and sculptures.

"My gosh," I mumbled. "How much is Mid-America paying him?"

"A lot more than cops get paid," Nick said.

"Maybe I should move into management," I said.

"His wife has that shop downtown," Nick pointed out.

"Yeah, but it's only been open a short while. It can't be earning this kind of money yet," I said. "It has to be Eric's bonuses. They must be huge. No way could he afford a place like this on a branch manager's salary alone."

A minute or two passed while we both stared at the houses.

"Why are you here questioning Eric?" I asked.

Nick shrugged. "Routine."

I doubted that was true and wondered if Nick suspected Eric of Jerry's murder, as I did.

"Have you found the suspect vehicle?" I asked. "Did it show up in the neighborhood? At a body shop?"

"No," Nick said. "Whoever has the car is either hiding it, or drove it up to the desert and burned it."

"Any other leads?" I asked.

Nick sighed. "Just a lot of people Donavan owed money to."

From what I knew of Jerry, that list must be a long one.

"You still haven't told me why you're here," Nick said.

If I'd felt closer to Nick I would have confided in him about my parents' marital problem.

"Mid-America might have to foreclose," I said, and nodded to the closest house. "I'm doing a property look-up."

"In the dark?"

It was really hard to get a lie over on a homicide detective. Still, I wasn't going to back down.

"It's just preliminary right now," I told him.

Nick grunted. I knew he didn't believe me.

It seemed like a good time to change the subject.

"I talked to my brother," I said. "He remembered Eric from high school. Said he had a psycho girlfriend. Do you remember her?"

Nick thought for a few seconds. "Doesn't sound familiar."

My brother and Eric, and maybe his girlfriend, were a year ahead of Nick, so I wasn't surprised he didn't remember her.

What happened to her? I wondered. Did she still think about him and wonder what-if?

"Want to get some dinner?" Nick asked.

Yes. Oh, yes. I wanted to go. I wanted to sit across the table from Nick and share a special evening with him. I wanted him to take me in his arms, hold me, make me feel safe and secure, and chase all my problems away.

I wanted him to tell me what had gone on with Katie Jo Miller back in high school so all those wonderful things could happen.

"No, thanks," I said.

Nick nodded slowly. I wondered if he was having

some of those same thoughts I'd just had. If so, he'd pushed them aside as I had done.

Or maybe he hadn't.

Nick leaned closer and pressed his palm against my cheek. My heart fluttered. He kissed me on the lips. Nice. Really nice.

"I haven't made-out in a car since high school," I whispered.

Nick trailed kisses along my jaw. "Want to get in the back seat?"

"Yes—no. No," I said, and eased away.

He sat back and gave me a half-grin.

"Stay out of trouble," Nick said, and climbed out of my car.

I started the engine and pulled away. Nick stood on the sidewalk, watching. I stared into the rearview mirror until he disappeared from view.

He'd told me to stay out of trouble. I had no intention of doing that. In fact, I just might cause some trouble.

I intended to find out if Mick Dudley actually existed.

* * *

I accessed the photo on my cell phone that I'd taken of Mick Dudley's loan application, and punched the address into my GPS. The route took me back toward Bonita, then south on the freeway for a twenty-minute drive to the town of Hayward. I exited and wound through the streets until my GPS announced that I'd arrived at my destination.

The neighborhood consisted of small, wood-frame houses built at least sixty years ago. Some of the owners had restored their homes back to their original beauty. Not this one, I saw as I stopped in front of what was supposed to be Mick Dudley's house. The porch roof sagged, two windows were broken out, and the yard was waist high. Nobody had lived here for a very long time.

My GPS next took me to what was supposed to be the machine shop a couple of miles away where Mick Dudley worked. The gravel of the parking lot crunched beneath my tires as I pulled in. My headlights lit up the building and illuminated a "for rent" sign that hung crooked in one of the dust-covered windows.

An icky feeling swept over me.

Either Mick Dudley actually existed and had intentionally given false information to obtain a loan he never planned to repay, or Eric Hunter had fabricated the customer and pocketed the loan proceeds.

While cheating the system by making loans and keeping the money was grounds for termination at Mid-America, it wasn't a criminal act—unless the company chose to bring charges, which wasn't likely due to the publicity—so I couldn't see how this related to Jerry's murder.

But maybe I didn't know everything yet.

I knew a place to check out.

I headed back to the freeway and drove north, then exited on State Street and made my way to Dayton Avenue, one of Santa Flores' main arteries. This section of the city changed from block to block, with upscale furniture and home décor stores, doctor and dentist offices giving way to tattoo parlors, discount T-shirt shops, hot dog stands with picnic tables out front, and bars. It was hardly the kind of neighborhood I felt safe in after dark, but tonight I was willing to risk it.

Only a half-dozen cars were in the parking lot of the

Buccaneer Bar when I pulled in. I found a space near the entrance under the lot's only security light and went inside.

The place was dark, lighted mostly by neon beer signs. Booths lined the back wall, the bar stood on the right, and tables and chairs were scattered in between. Everything looked worn and scarred. Whatever had inspired the owner to name the place the Buccaneer was no longer in evidence.

Two of the booths were occupied, as were a couple of tables; three guys sat at the bar watching a basketball game on the only TV. I slid onto a stool at the opposite end of the bar. The bartender walked over and frowned.

"I paid you this month, Dana," he said.

Francis Malloy was a big guy in his forties, with a shaved head and tattoos on both arms.

"I know," I said, and smiled. "I keep an eye on your account."

Francis had an account with Mid-America and had fallen behind on his payments a few months ago. I'd tried to work with him but he refused to return my calls—until I'd showed up here at the bar one night and confronted him.

I guess my courage in coming to a place like this had impressed Francis because he started making his payments pretty regularly after that. I'd stopped by the few times he'd fallen behind, and he'd always paid me out of the register.

That's how I happened to run into Jerry Donavan here. He'd been a regular. We'd chatted every time I'd come to collect Francis' payment.

"Beer?" Francis asked.

I was tempted but shook my head.

He frowned. "Don't tell me you're still on the

clock."

"Sort of," I said. "Did you hear about Jerry Donavan?"

Francis blew out a heavy breath. "Bad deal, all way around."

"Had he mentioned any problems lately?" I asked.

"Just the same old things. The ex-wives. The kids. Money. But, hell, everybody worries about that stuff."

I couldn't shake the feeling that there was a connection between Jerry and Eric that went well beyond Jerry's contract with Mid-America to do appraisal reports. I pulled out my cell phone and swiped the screen until I came to the photo taken the night of Eric's birthday celebration. It was a group shot, all of us leaning in and smiling while the waiter took our picture.

"How about this guy?" I asked, holding up my phone and pointing to Eric. "Has he been in, maybe?"

"That guy?" Francis chuckled. "He's way too pretty for a place like this."

So much for that idea.

I dropped my phone in my handbag and said, "Jerry had his share of problems, but who thought something like this could happen to him?"

"And just when he was turning things around," Francis said. He picked up a cloth and started polishing shot glasses. "He had a new girlfriend, you know."

"I didn't know," I said.

"Nice lady," he said. "Works at that flower shop down the block. She had him on the straight and narrow. I hadn't seen him in here in a couple of weeks."

I remembered then that Marsha had commented how Jerry was finally getting his life together. Misty, who'd known him for only a few weeks, had called him a nice guy.

Could Jerry have really changed?
And could it have gotten him killed?

Chapter 8

When I arrived at the office the next morning I found a note from Manny on my desk. He'd been called to a meeting with the district manager in Riverside and would be back after lunch. While Manny didn't keep a constant eye out to make sure I was working all day long, I was glad he wasn't there this morning because I had some distasteful personal business to handle.

I put in a call to the title company Mid-America did business with and ordered a property profile, a report that provided all sorts of information about a particular address. It was a routine request, one of the things I often did when trying to locate a customer who had skipped or if I was helping Manny with a possible foreclosure.

Only this time it was personal. I wanted information on the woman whose house my dad had gone to last night.

I asked the clerk at the title company to rush it and he promised he would. I was keyed up, anxious to know who this woman was that had gotten involved with my dad and ruined my parents' marriage.

The title company's idea of a rush request might take hours. But instead of pulling up my collection route and calling my customers, I decided to take care of another pressing personal matter.

Whoever had programmed Mid-America's computer system had built in the capability for any office to access the accounts in every other office. This came in handy when a customer wanted to make a payment in a different branch, which happened all the time.

I accessed the accounts in the Bonita branch and did a name search for Mick Dudley. The notion that Eric Hunter had made a loan to somebody who didn't really exist kept nagging at me. I couldn't stop thinking that it was somehow connected to Jerry's murder.

Mick Dudley's supposed account popped up on my computer screen. I did a double take. Yesterday afternoon, it had been past due. Now it showed a zero balance. The account had been paid in full this morning.

I sat back in my chair, staring at the screen.

Was this an incredible coincidence? I doubted it.

Eric knew I'd found the account yesterday; Gloria had told him about it. He'd probably gotten worried and paid it off to cover his tracks. I had a strong suspicion that if anyone looked for the actual paper file in the Bonita branch, it wouldn't be found.

I wondered if Gloria knew what Eric was up to. She'd looked as if she could claw out my eyes when she'd seen me pull the file yesterday. Maybe she was in on it.

The thing about making a bogus loan was that you couldn't make just one. If you were going to keep your misdeeds to yourself, undetected by other branch personnel or during routine visits from the district manager or the auditing team, payments had to be made on the account. This required another fraudulent loan. And it went on from there, like a pyramid scheme. Loan after loan, with some of the proceeds used to make payments on the existing loans, and the rest going into your own pocket.

No telling how many bogus loans Eric had made. Maybe this was the first but I doubted it—especially after seeing the magnificent home he and Lourdes lived in.

But still, I couldn't see a connection to Jerry's

murder.

A message from the title company appeared in my inbox. I clicked on the icons, and the pages of the property profile I'd ordered glided out of the printer on the credenza behind Manny's desk. I snatched them up and went back to my desk.

According to the profile, the house where my dad had been spending a great deal of time lately belonged to a woman named Lorna Pettigrew. She was the sole owner. She'd lived there for a little over a year. There were no liens or judgments recorded against the property and no mortgage, which meant that she'd either bought the house outright for cash, someone had purchased it for her, or somebody had died and left it to her.

I didn't have all the info I needed to get a credit report on her but I gave it a try. Something popped, much to my surprise. I'd only seen this woman from a distance beneath the feeble porch light, but I'd guessed her age at around fifty. The credit bureau report indicated I was right. It also showed that she had three credit cards, all with low balances, and had a history of excellent credit dating back several decades.

Something about seeing all this information about her made my blood boil. Then I started to feel sick. I grabbed my handbag and a file folder from the stack on my desk, and headed for the door.

"Manny wants me to do a property lookup for him," I called as I rushed past Inez's desk.

She said something but I ignored her and dashed outside.

* * *

I hit the freeway and drove mindlessly. There wasn't much traffic this time of day and the November weather was gorgeous, as always.

Life had a way of taking an ugly turn—no matter how good you thought your mojo was. Sometimes, maybe you had it coming. Other times, you were blindsided.

Honestly, this thing with my dad? I never saw it coming.

I transitioned onto another stretch of the freeway that ringed Santa Flores.

What would be really nice right now, what I'd truly appreciate, was someone I could confide in. Somebody who would listen. Spreading a burden around always made it easier to carry.

My best friend Jillian came to mind, but she was at work. She'd listen, if I called, but the problem was too big for a quick explanation over the phone.

Then Nick popped into my head. Nick? Oh, yes, Nick.

I felt myself relax at the thought of telling him my problem, seeing the worried, understanding expression on his face, feeling his arms around me as he gave me a hug that would make it all better.

But how could I do that? I'd been adamant about not allowing him to get close. I couldn't contact him now just because I had a problem and wanted him to do something that would make *me* feel better. That wouldn't be right.

Maybe pushing him away wasn't right either.

I changed lanes and aimed for the Dayton Avenue exit.

I wasn't up to dealing with my feelings for Nick right now. This problem with my parents was all I could manage, and I could think of only one way to handle it.

There was no way I was going to tell my mom what I'd

discovered—not until I'd talked to my dad first. I'd do that tonight. Maybe by then the sting of the whole thing might lessen.

Heading back to the office right now didn't seem appealing; I had an errand that would put it off for a while longer.

I cruised down Dayton Avenue, past the Buccaneer Bar—already there were two cars in the parking lot—and kept watch for the flower shop Francis had mentioned last night, the one where Jerry Donavan's new girlfriend worked. I spotted it and pulled into the lot.

The shop was crowded into a small plaza with a gift boutique, an ice cream parlor, and a used book store. Its windows displayed autumn-themed floral arrangements. Outside were brightly painted wooden carts filled with colorful flowers.

I parked and went inside, and wound my way through the green plants, vases, and gift items to the counter in the back. A gray-haired woman wearing a yellow apron was on the phone. She smiled, jotted something down and hung up.

"Hi," I said. "I'm looking for someone who knew Jerry Donavan. I understand she works here."

The woman's smile fell, and she drew back a little. Her gaze took in the skirt, blouse and blazer I had on. I figured she pegged me for a bill collector, which I was, of course, and I knew she was reluctant to admit to anything.

"My name is Dana Mackenzie," I explained. "I knew Jerry through my job at Mid-America. He did appraisals for us. I'd known Jerry for a long time and, well, I was there the morning it ... happened."

"How awful for you," she said softly. "That whole thing was awful. Just awful, wasn't it?"

"I know Jerry had a girlfriend who worked here," I said. "I thought she might want to … well, she might want to talk a bit."

My reason for coming here wasn't to offer comfort to Jerry's girlfriend, really, but to try and gain some insight into what was going on with him during the last few weeks of his life. And if that somehow led to his killer, I figured it would be okay with the girlfriend.

"That would be Charla," she said softly. "Wasn't that just awful? It was awful, wasn't it?"

"Awful," I agreed.

"I'll be right back," she said, and disappeared through the curtained doorway behind her.

A few minutes later Charla appeared. Her gray hair was pulled back in a ponytail and deep wrinkles cut grooves around her mouth and eyes. She looked as if life had been difficult for her.

"Dana?" She came forward and reached for my hand. "Oh, Dana, I'm so pleased to meet you. I feel like I know you. Jerry talked about you."

"He did?" I asked.

"Let's go outside," Charla said, and led the way out of the shop. We moved into the shade at the corner of the building, near the flower carts.

"Jerry knew how you helped out his friend Francis, at the bar," Charla said.

"I'm so sorry about what happened," I said. "I know this is a tough time for you."

Charla sighed and years of emotional wear and tear showed on her face.

"Things happen," she said, and forced a smile. "We have to trust in the Lord and know it's for the best. Part of His plan. Jerry would agree with that."

I wasn't so sure about that.

"I didn't know Jerry was involved in a church," I said.

"You're remembering the old Jerry," Charla said, her smile a little brighter now. "The new Jerry came to church with me every Sunday. I insisted. He was reluctant at first, but he came."

"He'd turned his life around?" I asked.

"Oh, yes, indeed he had," Charla said. "In the last few weeks he was atoning for all his sins. Confessing what he'd done wrong. Trying to make up for his mistakes. Even trying to patch up things with his children."

I flashed on Brooke and her mother Patricia in the verbal altercation with Marsha over Jerry's money that had required police intervention.

"How was that going?" I asked.

"Slowly," Charla admitted. "But Jerry was getting there. I know he would have had a wonderful relationship with those kids if he hadn't—"

She paused and tears pooled in her eyes.

"Any idea who might have done this to Jerry?" I asked.

"I can't imagine why anyone would do something like that," she said.

We were both quiet for a couple of minutes, then Charla drew in a breath and gave herself a shake.

"Thank you for coming by," she said. "And if you'd like to go to services, let me know. You can always find me here at the shop."

"I will," I said, and headed for my car.

I'd reached the front fender when I heard her call my name. I turned and saw her walking toward me. I met her halfway.

"There was one thing. I don't know if it means anything. Probably not, but well, you never know," Charla said. "I went to pick up Jerry one evening in that alley behind the strip mall. You know, where Jerry had his office? When I pulled in I saw him standing outside. He seemed to be arguing with a woman."

"When was this?" I asked.

"Last week. Tuesday," Charla said. "Tuesday nights are our prayer service."

"Did you recognize her?" I asked.

"I don't know any of Jerry's friends, not on sight, anyway. He told me about quite a few, like you and Francis at the bar. We associate with people from the church. But things got heated between them. Jerry saw me and must have said something, because she stormed off."

"What did she look like?" I asked.

"Oh, dear, my eyes aren't what they used to be, of course," she said. "But she was tall, trim, with long hair. Blonde hair."

"What did Jerry say about her?" I asked.

"He told me not to worry. Said it was nothing."

"Did you notice what sort of car she drove away in?" I asked.

Charla thought for a few seconds and shook her head. "Not really."

She glanced back at the flower shop. "I'd better get in there. Let me know if you want to go to church," she said, and hurried away.

Brooke had long blonde hair. I hadn't paid much attention to the car that she and Patricia drove away in the day of the confrontation outside the office. I had only a vague memory that it was dark. Small and dark. Like the vehicle that had killed Jerry.

Had Patricia learned of the argument between her daughter and her ex-husband? Had it been the final straw?

Maybe the reason I couldn't find a connection between Eric's bogus loan and Jerry's death was simple.

There wasn't one.

Chapter 9

I checked my watch as I started my car. Manny wasn't supposed to be back from his meeting in Riverside with the DM until after lunch, several hours from now, but there was always a chance he'd come back early. Since I'd left the office under false pretenses, I didn't want him to return and not find me there.

I dug my cell phone from my handbag and called the office, hoping Carmen would answer. She did.

"Is Manny back?" I asked.

"Not yet," she said. "You want me to leave a message for him?"

"No," I said. "I'll be back to the office soon."

"Okay," she said. "See you later—oh, wait. You got a message."

I cringed at the thought that Ronald had called me again, which I didn't feel so great about.

"A lady named Marsha called," Carmen said.

I hoped that meant she had some good news about the appraisals Jerry had been working on for us.

"Text me her number, would you?" I asked.

"Yeah—oh, got to run. Customer." She hung up.

I sat in the car for a few minutes until my cell phone chimed and the text with Marsha's phone number appeared on my screen. I called and she answered right away.

"Good news," Marsha said. "I have several of the appraisal reports that belong to Mid-America on my computer at home. I'm getting the photos printed out."

"That's great," I said. "Can I come by and pick them up?"

"I'll be at the office tomorrow," she said.

"Okay, I'll see you then," I said. "Thanks for—"

"Dana?"

Something about the way she said my name set my nerves on edge.

"A strange thing happened and I don't know what to do about it," Marsha said. "I was cleaning out Jerry's desk and I found money hidden in the bottom of a drawer. Over two grand. In cash."

That was a lot of money to leave lying around—especially when Jerry was having trouble paying his bills and keeping up with his alimony and child support.

"Where did it come from?" I asked.

"No idea. He was always paid by check. I handled his bank account," Marsha said. She paused for a bit then said, "I think the money should go to Patricia."

This, I hadn't expected.

Marsha rushed on. "I know, I know, she made a big scene and that daughter of hers threatened me, but let's face it, Jerry was no saint. Yes, he'd turned his life around these past few weeks but he put her through a lot."

I thought about it for a few seconds. Should I go along with giving Patricia the money even though I suspected her of running Jerry down in the alley?

"And she's got those teenagers," Marsha pointed out.

I decided that whether Patricia killed Jerry or not, her kids could still use the money.

"I agree," I said.

Marsha heaved a sigh. "I'm glad because, well, I'm kind of afraid to approach Patricia after what happened the other day. I was wondering if you'd take it to her."

—

82

This was hardly an enviable task—I wasn't all that crazy about approaching Patricia either—but I understood Marsha's concern.

"Sure," I said. "I'll pick up the money from you when I get the appraisal reports."

"You're a life saver, Dana. See you tomorrow," she said and hung up.

I started my car and pulled out of the parking lot but instead of heading south toward the office, I went north and turned right onto State Street.

Nobody kept that much money hidden in a desk drawer unless they were up to something. I thought about Eric and the fraudulent loan I'd discovered, and wondered again if Jerry was somehow connected to it. There was no way I could ever find out for sure, since I wasn't authorized to pull every file in the Bonita branch and check out the borrowers, but I knew somebody who would probably already know the truth.

I cruised down State Street for a few miles, passed the Bonita office, then turned onto Jackson Park. I swung into an apartment complex. Janine lived there. Not long ago when her car had been in the shop I'd given her a ride to work for a couple of days. We'd exchanged phone numbers back then, but I didn't want to call now. I was afraid she'd tell me not to come over.

I spotted her Kia, pulled in next to it, then left my car and headed for her apartment. The complex was huge and showing signs of aging, but was well maintained. There were lots of green belts, trees, and shrubs.

Her apartment was on the second floor. I climbed the stairs and knocked on her door. There was no noise from inside and I wondered if she was out for a walk or visiting a neighbor, or still in bed. I knocked again.

Finally I heard footsteps and a few seconds later the door opened a crack. Janine peeked out beneath the security chain.

"Feel like some company?" I asked.

Her gaze darted past me. "Are you alone?" she whispered.

I nodded. Janine hesitated for a few seconds, then pushed the door closed. I heard the rattle of the security chain and the door opened again.

"The police keep coming by," Janine said stepping back and wringing her hands. "They've been here twice already. I don't want to talk to them anymore."

"I don't blame you," I said, and walked inside. She closed the door behind me and slid the chain into place again.

The apartment was silent. No music played. I didn't hear the television.

From what I could see from the entryway, Janine had decorated her apartment as if she intended to live there for a while. She had nice furniture, plants, and pictures on the walls. Everything looked neat and clean, and well cared for.

I couldn't say the same for Janine. She had on sweat pants, a washed out T-shirt, and her hair was pulled up in a messy ponytail. Her face was puffy and her eyes were red. I wasn't sure if it was because she'd been crying, or not sleeping much.

I followed her into the living room. All the blinds were drawn, casting everything in dim light.

"How are you doing?" I asked.

"Not that great," she said, and gestured to the sofa. I sat down and she plopped into the chair across from me. "I keep seeing it over and over in my head. I can't make it stop."

Janine pressed her fingertips to her lips. They were shaking.

"That's terrible," I said, and was glad I hadn't been in Janine's place in the alley. I wouldn't want those pictures in my head for the rest of my life.

"And the nightmares." Janine clamped her palms against her head. "They won't stop."

Obviously, Janine had been deeply traumatized by witnessing Jerry's death. I remembered Nick's suggestion that she'd recognized the driver and I wondered if perhaps she had, and that knowledge had added to her distress.

Still, I couldn't imagine why she wouldn't just come out and say so if she knew—or suspected—who the driver was.

Janine leaned back in the chair and tears welled in her eyes. "The doctor gave me some pills. They aren't helping."

I'd come here hoping Janine would have some input on what was going on with Eric and the possibility that he was making fraudulent loans. I could see that she was emotionally fragile. I didn't want to make things worse.

Janine folded her hands and gazed toward the window. Since the blinds were closed she couldn't see out, but she kept staring.

A few awkward moments dragged by and I was sorry I'd come. I wanted to leave, but I didn't think I should just walk out.

"Can I get you something?" I asked. "Do you need anything?"

Another minute passed. She kept staring at the blinds.

"It was a four." Finally, Janine turned to me. "I

remembered it when I woke up this morning. It was a four. The license plate. It started with a four."

California license plates started with a number, followed by three letters and three numbers. That first number was an indicated of when the vehicle was originally purchased, or the last time it changed hands. A car with a plate that began with a four had been on the road for a long time, around fifteen years old.

"I should tell the police," Janine murmured. "I don't want to talk to them anymore."

I didn't see this as a clue that would break the case but maybe it would help.

"Would you like me to tell them for you?" I asked.

Janine didn't say anything. Her gaze was fixed on a spot across the room. I decided to try and lighten the mood.

"The office's Thanksgiving food drive is creeping along," I said. "But Inez will pull it together in plenty of time."

That seemed to snap Janine out of her stupor.

"My uncle Saul manages the Vons store on State Street," she said. "He's donating all kinds of food. I just have to pick it up."

"That explains why I didn't find a list of donors in your desk," I said. "Eric asked me to check on it and follow up—"

"What?" Janine lurched to her feet, screaming. "You're working *there*? In that office?"

I jumped up. "Well, yes, but—"

"You have to get out of there!" Janine shook her head frantically. "That last girl, the one before Misty, she got told to quit—*or else.* And I told Misty to mind her own business. I told her. I told her not to look at him.

—

86

Not to talk to him unless she absolutely had to. You didn't talk to him, did you? Did you?"

"You mean Eric?" I asked.

"Yes!"

What had I stumbled on? Something far worse than a possible fraudulent loan? I had no idea where this was going.

"Eric told that last girl to quit or else?" I asked.

"Not him! Her!" Janine shrieked. "She thought that girl was flirting with him. She comes to the office all the time. She sees everything that goes on."

"Lourdes?" I asked.

"She's crazy!"

I was beginning to think Janine was the crazy one.

So Lourdes was protective of her relationship with Eric. Maybe she had good reason. Maybe there was something going on between him and the girl who'd worked there before Misty. Maybe he'd cheated on her, or she suspected him of cheating on her now.

Sure, confronting an office employee and threatening her if she didn't resign wasn't right. But was it crazy?

I thought about Patricia. I thought about my own mom. How far would any woman go when it came to dealing with an unfaithful husband?

"Everything is going to be okay," I said to Janine, in the most soothing voice I could muster. "I'll talk to Misty. I'll make sure she stays out of trouble with Eric and Lourdes. And believe me, I don't want to go back and work in that branch ever again."

Janine drew in big breaths. "Promise?"

"Promise," I said and drew a little cross over my heart.

"Okay," she said. "Okay."

She seemed better but I was worried about leaving her alone.

"Does your mom or somebody live nearby?" I asked.

Janine nodded.

"Maybe you should call her, ask her to come over."

She gulped hard. "Mom said I should hire an attorney. But I'll be okay. Really, I'll be fine."

I wasn't so sure about that, but I couldn't force her to call someone.

"If you need anything, let me know," I said.

Janine drew in another big breath, held it for a few seconds, and let it out slowly.

"Thanks," she said.

As I left the apartment, I heard Janine lock the door and slide the security chain into place. I thought I should call Nick and tell him what she'd remembered about the suspect vehicle.

I also thought about how life had turned around for Eric. He'd hooked up with a psycho girlfriend back in high school and later had found a wife who loved him deeply, even if she sometimes showed it in a kind of crazy way.

Seemed Eric's luck had been outstanding.

Chapter 10

I knew there was no way Janine would be up to collecting the Thanksgiving food donations and getting them delivered to the Bonita office, so I took on the task. I figured it was the decent thing to do—plus, it delayed my return to work by at least another half hour.

Janine's uncle Saul at the Vons grocery store was really nice when I explained about Janine and that I was there to pick up the donation. He looked at my business card, then asked one of the bag boys to cart everything to my car.

While the guy packed my trunk and back seat full of cases of canned beans, peas, corn, and mixed vegetables, Saul talked about what Janine had been through witnessing the hit-and-run. I thanked him for the donation and left.

I didn't know how Eric planned to get the donation to the food bank in L.A.—Corporate had left it to the branches to figure it out—so I called the Bonita office as soon as I pulled away from Vons.

"Eric's not here," Misty told me, when she answered the phone.

"Let him know I picked up the canned goods donation Janine got," I said. The last Eric knew, Janine hadn't done anything about the food drive. I figured I'd explain everything when I dropped off the donation.

"Cool," Misty said. "I'll tell Eric as soon as he gets back."

Janine's screams echoed in my mind.

"Just put a note on his desk, okay?" I said.

She promised she would and we hung up.

I continued down State Street, then pulled into the turning lane at Fleming Avenue and waited for the light to change.

Honestly, I couldn't imagine how knowing the age of the car that had run down Jerry would do much to solve the case. Nick already knew it was small and dark; knowing it was old couldn't add anything to locating it.

Still, I thought I should pass along the info. I called Nick. His voicemail picked. Hearing him speak always made my heart do a little flip-flop. I wondered at my true motive for sharing the info. I left a message asking him to call me.

When I turned onto Fifth Street and into the Mid-America parking lot, I spotted Nick standing near the building. My heart did a bigger flip-flop.

He looked handsome, dressed in a navy blue sport coat, a pale blue shirt, and a gray and blue stripped necktie. Nick looked handsome in anything.

As I swung into a parking space, he walked over and opened my door.

"Throwing a dinner party?" he asked, eyeing the cases of food in my backseat.

"Just me and a few hundred of my closest friends," I said, getting out of the car.

"And my invitation?" he asked.

"It's in the mail," I told him.

Nick grinned. I loved Nick's grin. I just stood there for what felt like an hour, staring at him. He didn't seem to mind. He seemed to enjoy staring back.

"So," he finally said, breaking whatever crazy spell was between us. "You called?"

"I did," I said, and it took another few seconds for me to remember why. "I talked to Janine Ferris."

Nick's gorgeous grin started to morph into his cop grimace, but I cut him off.

"I went to see her about the Thanksgiving food donation," I said, and gestured to my backseat as evidence.

Really, that wasn't the reason I'd gone but there was no point in sharing my suspicions about Eric with him. I had no proof, plus making a loan to a non-existent customer wasn't something a homicide detective could do anything about. I had no proof that Patricia had run down Jerry, either. All I had was suspicion, and what good would that do Nick's investigation?

"Janine remembered something about the car that ran down Jerry," I said. "The license plate started with the number four."

"So it was old," he said, and I was sure I could see him calculating the approximate age of the vehicle, as I had done. "Did she remember any more of the plate number?"

I shook my head. "That's it."

Nick stewed on this for a minute, then frowned. "Why didn't she tell me?"

"She doesn't like you."

Nick drew back a little. He wasn't accustomed to a female who didn't like him.

"You like me, though. Right?" he asked. He grinned again. "And remember, it's a crime to lie to a police officer."

Yes, I liked him. He liked me, too. We both knew it. But that wasn't the issue between us.

"I've always been truthful with you," I said. "That's more than I can say for you."

The playfulness left Nick's face. I could see that my words had hurt him, and I didn't like doing that. But he'd hurt me, too, by not coming clean about him and Katie Jo.

Why wouldn't he just tell me? Why was he keeping it a big secret? Especially when he knew how much it meant to me to know the truth? It was the one thing that was keeping us apart.

Nick just looked at me, and for a few seconds I thought—I hoped—he would explain himself and finally put this whole issue behind us.

But he didn't.

"Thanks for the information about the car," he said, then walked away.

* * *

"You should break up with him," Jillian said.

I looked across the table at my best friend and knew she was right.

"I know," I said. "But—"

We were sitting in a little café on Sixth Street where we'd met for dinner. Outside, it was dark but twinkle lights sparkled in the trees and shrubs that were planted at the edge of the sidewalk. This area of Santa Flores had been revitalized over the past couple of years, bringing in upscale shops and restaurants that gave the street a Tuscan vibe.

"But nothing," Jillian said. "You have to break up with Ronald. You're involved with him for all the wrong reasons."

"I know," I said again. "But he's good looking, and all the holiday parties are coming up."

Jillian gave me a look that only a best friend can get away with and asked, "Can you honestly tell me you have any feelings for him? Does he mean anything to you? Do

92

you even think about him during the day?"

I realized that when I'd been upset about my dad's affair and had wished for someone to talk to about it, I'd never thought about turning to Ronald. It didn't make me feel so great about myself.

"You're right, you're right," I admitted.

We were quiet for a few minutes while I finished my salad and Jillian ate the last of her sandwich.

"This is really about Nick, isn't it?" she said.

I pushed my plate away, annoyed.

"What's the matter with him? Why won't he just tell me the truth about what happened with Katie Jo?" I asked. "He knows how much this means to me."

"Are you sure you really want to know?" she asked.

"Of course, I want to know. It's driving me crazy not knowing."

"Consider this," Jillian said. "If Nick confesses, if he tells you it wasn't him, if he says he didn't get Katie Jo pregnant, will you believe him?"

"Oh," I mumbled, stunned. "I guess I hadn't thought about it."

"Well, think about it," Jillian told me. "Nick knows how much is riding on this. He knows this issue is what's keeping you two apart. He likes you, he wants to date you, he wants you to get over this whole thing. Where's his incentive to tell you anything except what you want to hear?"

"You have a point," I admitted.

"Or," Jillian went on. "What if Nick tells you he did it, he got Katie Jo pregnant, made her have that abortion, then dumped her and left town? How are you going to feel about him then? Are you going to be okay with everything, put it behind you, start dating him like

93

everything is great between you? You'll know the truth—but is that a truth you really want to know?"

"Jeez," I muttered and sat back in my chair.

Jillian had made lots of good point. They were all true and all something important to think about—but none of them actually resolved this situation with Nick.

"No matter what he says," Jillian said, "will it really make things okay between you? Really make you happy?"

I slumped in the chair. "All along I thought that if I knew the truth, I'd be okay. But now …"

I looked across the table at Jillian. "I hate you."

She smiled, as only a best friend can. "I know."

"Let's get out of here," I said.

I signaled the waitress and she brought our check. Jillian grabbed it.

"This is on me," she said, handing over her credit card, "since I ruined your life tonight."

The waitress left and I was about to ask Jillian about her weekend plans when she leaned forward and nodded toward the door.

"Don't you know her? I saw her in a photo on your Facebook page," she said.

I turned and saw Lourdes Hunter standing at the counter, talking to the hostess. She had on a maxi skirt with a slit up the side, boots, a cowl neck sweater and chunky jewelry. Her blonde hair was pulled into an elegant up-do. Lourdes looked fantastic, as she had the night I'd met her at Eric's birthday celebration.

I told Jillian her name and how I knew her.

"Lourdes owns a shop down the block," I said. "It's called Elegant and Artful: Distinctive Décor for the Discriminating Decorator, or something like that."

"My mom shops there." Jillian lowered her voice.

"She says everything costs a fortune."

"I need to talk to her," I said, and left the table.

My car was packed full of canned goods that belonged to the Bonita office and since Lourdes was standing right there, I wanted to make arrangements with her to take the donation to her house tonight and let Eric figure out what to do with it.

"Hi," I said, as I approached her still waiting at the register.

Lourdes spared me a cool glance and said, "Hello."

"I'm Dana Mackenzie," I said. "I work at Mid-America's Santa Flores branch."

"What?" Lourdes seemed distracted and slightly annoyed that I'd bothered her.

"We met at Eric's birthday celebration," I said.

"Oh. Oh, yes, of course." Lourdes forced a smile. "Yes, I remember you now."

I wasn't sure she really recalled meeting me that evening, but she was trying hard to pretend she did.

Lourdes seemed to be trying hard to pretend at more than that.

That night in the restaurant at Eric's birthday celebration, we'd been seated at opposite ends of a long table so I hadn't seen her up close. Now, I could see that she'd gone heavy on her makeup trying to conceal lines around her eyes and mouth. Her nose looked as if it were unnaturally straight and her lips were a little fuller than they should have been.

Lourdes leaned over the counter and looked back into the kitchen, anxious for her take-out order, I guessed.

"I was helping out in Eric's branch this week and I collected the canned goods for the food drive," I said. "It's all in my car. Can I drop by your house and put them in your garage?"

"What?" Lourdes whipped around. "No."

For someone who was so involved with her husband's job, I was surprised and taken slightly aback.

She saw my reaction and turned on a bright smile, as if she'd flipped a mental switch.

"Of course you could. It would be no problem at all—usually." Lourdes relaxed her stance and gave me a conspiratorial smile. "But our garage door is broken. I've been after Eric for a week now to get it fixed, but you know how men can be. He just hasn't gotten around to it yet. Just take the donation to the office tomorrow. I'll tell Eric to expect you."

"Okay, thanks," I said.

I saw that Jillian was rising from our table so I went outside to wait. The air was cool, making for a crisp autumn evening.

I wasn't thrilled about having to go back to the Bonita branch tomorrow to drop off the canned goods, and the broken garage door excuse seemed a little too convenient. I wondered if something else was going on. Either way, there was nothing I could do about it.

Jillian came outside. "Want to go shopping?"

"No, I can't tonight," I said.

I had to go see my dad.

* * *

"We need to talk," I said.

Dad looked surprised to see me—which I'm sure he was, given that I'd pulled across the driveway blocking in his truck just as he walked out of the house, then hopped out and confronted him.

I'd waited down the street for him to come out, dreading the conversation, slightly sick to my stomach and wishing I hadn't eaten that salad with Jillian earlier this evening.

"Sure," Dad said, following me to the other side of the house. The street light burned softly, but was bright enough that I could see his face, read his expression.

I hadn't told Mom anything that I'd discovered about Dad and Lorna Pettigrew. I wanted to learn the whole story myself, then decide how best to tell her.

"What's wrong with your mother?" Dad asked. "Cold sandwiches for dinner three nights in a row. What's going on?"

I'd rehearsed what I intended to say to Dad on the drive over. I'd tried to come up with the best approach, something that wouldn't sound harsh and judgmental, hoping he would explain—or confess—everything. Now, seeing him, knowing Mom was in the house devastated that he was leaving again, I couldn't hold back.

"You're cheating on her," I said. "What do you expect?"

Dad went white. His eyes bulged.

"She knows," I said. "She knows about the money you took out of your savings account. She knows you've been lying to her every night. She knows you haven't been going to Leo's house to work on his car."

He just stared at me.

Tears welled in my eyes. "I know, too. I know where you've been going. I know her name, where she lives. I know everything about her. I saw you there, Dad. I saw you go into her house."

"I have to talk to your mother."

Dad tried to slip around me, but I blocked him.

"She's already upset," I told him. "I don't want you making it worse."

"My God," Dad moaned. "She thinks that? She really things I'm cheating on her?"

"Aren't you?" I asked.

"No! No, of course not. I love your mother," he said. "Listen, this is all a mistake. Leo knows this woman. Her name is Lorna something. Her husband divorced her a year ago. She got a settlement. She bought a new house. She wanted new closets. Those big closet systems. Leo was going to install it for her, but his elbow is acting up. I told him I'd do it. She's paying me a small fortune."

"Then why didn't you tell Mom?" I demanded. "Why did you lie to her?"

"So I could surprise her with a cruise," Dad said. "Our anniversary. I wanted to do something special for her this year. I took the money out of our savings to put down the deposit. Look. I've got it right here."

Dad pulled his wallet out of his back pocket, flipped through it and held out a slip of paper. It was a receipt from a travel agency.

"So, you're not …?" I gulped hard. "You didn't …?"

"No, baby, I'm not cheating on your mother," he said.

Dad put his arms around me and pulled me close.

I burst out crying.

Chapter 11

"I saw Janine yesterday," I said, as I sat down in the chair beside Manny's desk.

Around us, the office was quiet. I'd purposely waited until Inez left for lunch to talk with Manny.

"She's a real mess," I said.

He shook his head. "Who can blame her?"

"I picked up the Thanksgiving food donation Janine arranged. I need a longer lunch hour so I can drop it off with Eric," I said.

Manny nodded. "Sure. No problem."

One of the things I liked most about Manny was that he was agreeable when it came to things like that. I decided to push my luck a little further.

"And I'm going to check on the appraisal reports, too" I said.

"Inez has been pacing the floor waiting for those things, driving us all crazy."

"Crazier than usual," I added.

Manny chuckled. "Sure. Take a longer lunch if you can get your hands on them."

With a somewhat leisurely afternoon ahead of me, I got my handbag from my desk and left the office. In my car, I headed north on Fleming Avenue anxious to drop off the canned goods at the Bonita branch.

My suspicion that Eric had made at least one fraudulent loan bothered me more and more. I was going to have to say something, I decided as I turned onto State

Street. After I delivered the food donations and felt certain I'd never have to work in Eric's branch again—whether Janine returned or Mid-America hired her replacement—I would say something to Manny.

Nobody liked a snitch, but I knew I'd be doing the right thing by ratting out Eric. Call it my attempt at justice—and Eric's bad mojo.

Of course, I still didn't see how it tied to Jerry's death—and maybe it didn't. Maybe my suspicion about Patricia had been right. Jerry's insurance money would go a long way toward supporting three teenagers.

I swung into the strip mall and drove into the alley behind the building. Instead of parking in a space, I pulled up alongside the rear entrance to the Mid-America office. I called Misty on my cell phone and asked her to unlock the door for me. A few minutes later, it was opened by Eric.

"Janine managed quite a contribution," I said, getting out of the car. "I talked to Lourdes last night and she—"

"You saw Lourdes?" he asked. There was an edge to his voice, as if I'd gone behind his back.

"I ran into her at the café down the street from her shop," I explained. "I wanted to bring the food by your house but she said your garage door was broken."

"Of course," Eric said, and looked relieved—about what I wasn't sure.

Misty came outside and the three of us stacked the cases of canned goods in the stockroom.

"Eric? You have a phone call," Gloria called from the office.

He waved and left. I did the same.

I didn't get into my car, though. Instead, I called

Marsha. She answered right away and said that she was in Jerry's office. I told her I was out back. We hung up and a minute later the rear door of the insurance company opened. Marsha stepped outside.

"I put all the appraisal reports in there," she said, passing me a large manila envelope. "Oh, and here's this."

She dug in the pocket of her jeans and came up with a wad of bills rolled up and secured with a rubber band.

"Still no idea where it came from?" I asked.

"None," Marsha said.

"I'll give it to Patricia," I promised.

"I found her address and phone number. It's in the envelope with the appraisals," Marsha said.

I wasn't looking forward to visiting Patricia. Hopefully she—or her daughter—wouldn't run me down in their driveway when they saw me get out of my car.

Marsha went back inside and I got into my Honda. I tucked the wad of cash inside my cosmetic bag. I didn't like walking around with so much money, especially when it didn't belong to me, and I was anxious to get rid of it.

I pulled the appraisal reports out of the manila envelope and found Patricia's contact info paper clipped to the one on top. I punched her address into my cell phone GPS and saw that she lived off Clayton Boulevard on the other side of town, completely out of my way. I'd cleared an extended lunch hour with Manny, so I decided I could run the errand on company time and he'd be none the wiser. I could also avoid stink-eye from Inez by presenting the appraisal reports she'd been wringing her hands about for days.

I flipped through the reports and saw that there were more of them that I was expecting. I looked closer and realized that Marsha had given me the appraisal reports for the Bonita branch, too.

Eleven of them, I counted. Wow, no wonder Eric was Mid-America's golden boy. The company standard was ten home equity loans per month for every branch— on top of all the personal loans each branch made. The month was more than half over and Eric still had this many equity loans going. Add these eleven to all the loans he'd already done this month and I could see why the profit he generated was among the highest in the company.

I separated the reports for our two offices into piles on my passenger seat and picked up my cell phone to call Misty and ask her to unlock the back door again. The address of one of the properties caught my eye. It was a house in my parents' neighborhood.

I'd lived in the home my parents' still owned since I was a kid. It was a quiet area of well-built houses that still showed pride of ownership. Sure, it was kind of old now but it had held up well over the years.

I knew the area. My mom and dad had taken me trick-or-treating, holding my hand to cross the street. I'd ridden my bicycle with my friends, and I'd learned to drive there. So, just for gee-whiz, I checked the value that Jerry had given the property when he'd done his appraisal.

"What the ...?" I mumbled.

I looked again at the street address, matched it to my knowledge of the neighborhood, and checked the value once more.

"No way," I said.

The value Jerry had given the home was higher— much higher—than it should have been. Tens of thousands of dollars more. But how could that be?

I flipped through the other appraisal reports and spotted three that were located in neighborhoods I was familiar with. Again, the values Jerry had assigned were out of whack, far higher than was reasonable for the areas.

How could Jerry have made that kind of mistake? What was he thinking?

Inez would have a complete hissy-fit if the appraisals Jerry had done for the Santa Flores branch were over-inflated—and nobody wanted to be around if that happened. I grabbed the appraisal reports for our branch and flipped through them. There were only three and I knew two of the neighborhoods. The values seemed okay to me.

None of this made sense. What had happened with the appraisals Jerry had done for Eric? Why would the values be so unreasonably high?

I gasped aloud as I realized what was going on. Jerry had deliberately overstated the values of the houses for the appraisals Eric had ordered.

The amount of money Mid-America could loan was based on the appraised value, so the higher the value, the bigger the loan. The bigger the loan, the more profit the branch earned. More profit equaled a bigger monthly bonus for the manager.

Another minute passed while I mulled everything over in my head, then it all fell into place.

Eric and Jerry were in on a scam together.

Eric had made at least one—and probably more—fraudulent loan. He'd used part of the proceeds to pay Jerry cash under the table for inflating the property values which, I suspected, was the source of the money Marsha had found hidden in his desk drawer.

With the higher property values, Eric made more and bigger loans, and earned huge monthly bonuses.

It was quite a scheme the two of them had going.

Eric was the darling of Mid-America, his branch's profit was high, as was his monthly bonus and his potential to get promoted up the corporate ladder. Jerry had made out well, too.

I slouched in my seat and drummed my fingers on the steering wheel.

So much for my theory that Eric had murdered Jerry. They were partners in a very lucrative, though unethical and deceitful, business arrangement. If anything, Eric would want to keep Jerry alive.

That left Patricia, the ex-wife. In theory, she was looking pretty good as a suspect right now.

And I was on my way to see her.

* * *

When I woke this morning I'd had a text message from Mom. "Huge misunderstanding," it had read, and was followed by two rows of smiley faces. I'd smiled too.

I hadn't talked to Mom today, and going to see her right now seemed like a wonderful idea. With what I'd just discovered about Eric and Jerry and what I suspected Patricia of doing, visiting my Mount Rushmore mom was exactly what I needed.

Pulling out of the alley, I circled the strip mall and turned left onto State Street. I turned up my CD player and buzzed down my window, hoping the beat of the music and the wind in my hair would chase away my troubles.

That didn't happen.

As if I didn't have enough on my mind, Ronald popped into my head.

Tonight was the special date he'd planned for us. He was a really nice guy, in a lot of ways. I'd wanted a sure-thing for all the upcoming holiday parties, which was selfish of me—although I'd hoped we'd eventually click.

But he wasn't the right guy for me. I guess we'd been doomed from the start.

Nick flew into my head. Had we been doomed from the start, too? Or was I being selfish again? Was my insistence that he reveal something from our distant past—ignoring his desire to keep it to himself—another example?

I turned onto my parents' street and pulled to a stop at the curb in front of their house. Another selfish thought came to me. Now that the misunderstanding between Mom and Dad had been cleared up, maybe Mom could help me sort out this thing with Nick.

The house was quiet when I let myself in. A delicious aroma filled the air—another sign that Mom was happy again. I followed it into the kitchen and saw the crock pot on the counter. Inside was a savory roast.

"Mom?" I called. "Mom?"

I got no answer so I headed down the hallway. I didn't see her anywhere, so I opened the door that led into the garage, thinking she was out there doing the laundry. Her car was gone.

Seemed my timing wasn't so good. I figured she might have run to the store for something quick, and since I had an extra-long lunch hour today, I decided to wait around for a while.

I ventured into the family room and switched on the TV. Dad had recently upgraded to a flat screen, but other than that everything had been the same for years. It was a comfortable room, filled with lots of memories.

Among the books on the built-in unit beside the fireplace, Mom had placed framed photos of Rob and me as we grew up—both of us in pajamas beside the Christmas tree; me with my two front teeth missing; Rob proudly displaying his first driver's license. There were photos of the four of us squeezed into one shot on the beach, at Disneyland, and with Rob and me in our cap and gown at our high school graduations.

My gaze traveled to the bottom row of the bookcase and I spotted a stack of yearbooks from Eastside High School. Mom had kept them for us. Somewhere, she'd also stored our tassels and graduation announcements.

I pulled out the yearbook from Rob's senior year and flipped through the pages. But instead of looking for Rob's photo, I turned to the junior class and found Nick's picture. My heart did a bigger than usual flip-flop.

Memories of Nick exploded in my head. Tall, good looking, football star, charmer.

I'd crushed on him big-time back then and, really, I'd been kind of jealous when he started dating my best friend Katie Jo. Then all that stuff had happened between them and I'd been crushed in a completely different way.

Seemed Nick and I weren't meant to be together back in high school, but we'd found each other several weeks ago and we'd felt a spark. If it hadn't been for Nick's involvement with Katie Jo, would we have gotten together back then? Stayed together?

Maybe all high school romances were destined for the memory scrap heap.

That made me think of Eric Hunter and his psycho girlfriend that my brother had mentioned. I figured Eric had been relieved to rid himself of her, but maybe she was the lucky one, given what Eric was doing now.

I turned a few more pages in the yearbook and found Eric's picture. He was a good looking man now, and he'd been a good looking guy back in the day. His features were harder, more angular now, as men got when they aged. Still, he was a head-turner.

I wondered what a reportedly psycho high school girl had to look like to be able to snare a hot guy like Eric. High school was about appearances, if nothing else. I thought back to my conversation with Rob, trying to remember the girl's name. Nora? No, it was Nola. Nola something.

I searched through the photos and found only one girl named Nola. Nola Miles.

She was attractive, but only a minor difference in her gene alignment would have made her beautiful. Her nose was a little wide, and chin was just a bit recessed. I could see why Eric had been attracted to her, though. Blonde hair, big eyes, and a beguiling smile that the photographer had easily captured.

A smile that looked very familiar.

I studied the photo for a long time, thinking and wondering where I'd seen her before. I'd lived in Santa Flores my whole life and Nola Miles probably still lived here too, so I might have seen her anywhere—the dentist's office, grocery store, at the mall, maybe.

Still, none of that seemed right.

She wouldn't look the same now, of course. She would have aged, changed her style. Maybe she'd even had some work done. I knew she wouldn't have been happy with her nose. I imagined it shaped differently, and how beautiful it would make her. The image of her in my mind morphed until I pictured her differently.

And I recognized her.

"Oh … my … God …," I mumbled.

I pulled my cell phone from the pocket of my pants and scrolled to the photo taken the night of Eric's birthday celebration. I laid it alongside the picture of Nola Miles in the yearbook.

Eric hadn't dumped his girlfriend after high school. He'd married her.

Chapter 12

I knew Nick had checked the DMV records to determine if a small black car was registered to everyone who might be involved with Jerry's murder—Eric, Gloria, Misty, Janine, his ex-wives, and probably Marsha. If he'd come up with anything, he would have told me. Nick would want me to know about, and be careful of, a possible murderer.

But I was certain Nick hadn't checked for a small black car registered to a Nola Miles.

I drove away from my parents' house with the high school yearbook photo looming large in my head.

No doubt about it, Eric's high school girlfriend was now Lourdes Hunter. Maybe that was her middle name; it wasn't listed under her photo. Maybe she'd made it up because she liked it and thought it fit her new image, after having her nose and chin fixed.

Whatever the reason, Lourdes had gone by a different name some fifteen years ago when the small black car that had run down Jerry had been new. It was possible Lourdes had purchased that car. It was possible she'd kept it all these years, never changed her name on the registration after she and Eric were married, and still owned it—also making it possible that I'd been right all along and Eric had killed Jerry.

The only way I could confirm my suspicion was to check the DMV records. I had no way of doing that.

But Nick did.

I turned onto State Street and headed for the freeway entrance.

I didn't want to call Nick. I didn't want to talk to him. We'd parted on bad terms the last time we were together and he'd made no attempt to contact me, to talk out our situation, or to try and make things better. He'd done nothing. This didn't inspire me to turn to him, confide in him, or share info.

Fortunately, I knew somebody who would help.

As I merged onto the freeway, I activated my Bluetooth and called Slade.

Slade worked for Quality Recovery, the company Mid-America—and I—turned to when we were forced to repossess a customer's car. Slade was one of their agents, known less politically correct as a repo guy.

He was ex-Air Force Special Ops. He was a big guy, well over six feet tall and very muscular. His wore his blond hair cut short. I figured his age at around thirty. He had an earring. Tattoos, too, I guessed, but I'd never seen any. Not that I hadn't wished I could look.

These repo guys were badass dudes, in it for the rush. Things could get crazy during a recovery. The cops might show up. A nosy neighbor might try to intervene. The vehicle owner might take offense to seeing his car being towed away and come out swinging—or shooting.

Quality Recovery was a part-time gig for Slade. I didn't know what he did when he wasn't picking up vehicles—nobody else seemed to know, either—but mercenary work in South America and anti-terrorism in the Middle East were definite possibilities.

I'd known Slade since I started the job at Mid-America. We'd kept it professional—even the time he ended up spending the night at my apartment.

Slade knew people. I was certain he could find out whether Lourdes Hunter, née Nola Miles, had a fifteen-year-old small black car registered to her.

"Hey," Slade said, when he answered my call.

"How's it going?" I asked.

"Cool," he said.

Slade wasn't exactly a big talker.

"Have you got time for some company?" I asked.

"Always," Slade said. "Staking out a Caddie. Taco Bell. Serrano and Third."

"I'll be there in a few," I said.

Slade didn't answer, just hung up.

I took the Serrano Avenue exit and drove a few miles west to Third Street, and spotted Slade in a black Blazer backed into a space at the Taco Bell on the corner. I parked and climbed in on the passenger side.

"Hey," he said.

"Hey," I said.

His brief remarks were contagious.

What Slade lacked in conversational skills he made up for in rugged good looks. Today he had on black jeans, black boots, and a black T-shirt.

"So you're waiting for a Caddie to show up?" I asked, as I gazed out the windshield.

He nodded toward the office building in the adjoining lot. "The guy's an accountant. Didn't make his payments. Dumbass."

Once Slade spotted the vehicle he'd call Quality Recovery and a tow truck team would immediately head this way. They worked fast. They would hook up the car and drive away in minutes, long before the accountant in his office knew what was happening. I'd seen Slade in action. Impressive.

"What's up?" he asked.

"I'm trying to find out if a woman named Nola Miles has a small black car registered in her name. Old. The plate starts with a four," I said.

He didn't hesitate, just picked up his cell phone from the seat between us and punched a number. Having a connection with a clerk at the DMV benefited Quality Recovery, although it wasn't anything official. I suspected cash changed hands in the DMV parking lot after the close of business.

Slade explained what he needed to whoever answered the phone. His gaze bounced between the office building parking lot and me while he held the phone to his ear and waited.

"So who is she?" he asked.

I wasn't all that anxious to share my suspicion about Eric. Not that Slade would have told me to butt out, as Nick would have. I just didn't want to make that kind of accusation until I had more info. But I wasn't going to lie to Slade.

"A friend of mine was killed. Hit and run," I said.

"Not cool," he said, shaking his head.

"I think this car might be involved," I said.

Slade turned to me, ignoring the parking lot and the Caddie he was watching for.

"You staying out of trouble on this?" he asked.

"Sure," I said, then added, "as much as I can."

"Call the cops?" he asked.

"If it pans out," I said.

"Thinking of checking it out yourself?"

Slade picked now to start being chatty?

"I just need to verify the owner of the vehicle," I said. "For now."

He gave me a long, hard look. I thought he intended to say something more but the DMV clerk must have come back on the line because Slade pressed the cell phone closer to his ear.

He listened for a few seconds then said, "Cool," and ended the call.

"Black Ford Fiesta," Slade said. "Registered to your gal on Dorchester Street in Maywood."

Eric and Lourdes lived on that street. The car that had struck Jerry as described by Janine matched the description of the vehicle registered to Lourdes in her previous persona of Nola Miles.

My stomach twisted into a knot

I imagined Eric leaving for work that morning in the little Ford, parking near the entrance of the alley, waiting for the door to the insurance office to open, watching for Jerry to walk outside. Then revving up the engine, slamming the accelerator, racing down the alley.

I guess Slade read something in my expression.

"You cool with this?" he asked.

I wasn't, but I said, "I'm okay."

"Calling the cops now?" he asked. "That detective? Travis?"

Slade had met Nick a few weeks ago during an incident outside the Mid-America office. Apparently he'd picked up on something between Nick and me; he'd never mentioned it until now.

"Sure," I told him.

Slade gave me another hard look.

"Want backup?" he asked.

"Cool," I said.

"Let's roll."

Slade started the Blazer and we drove away.

* * *

Slade cruised down Dorchester Street. The landscaping was lush and the grass was green—folks in the area could afford to run their sprinklers year round. Harvest-themed wreaths hung on most of the doors, and corn stalks, pumpkins, and golden mum plants decorated the porches.

The neighborhood was quiet. No kids played outside, nobody walked dogs.

Eric's place was the third house from the corner. There were no cars parked out front but I didn't expect to see any. I'd left Eric at the Bonita office a short while ago and Lourdes was at her shop on Sixth Street.

On the drive over I'd pieced most everything together—except for Eric's motive for killing Jerry. The scheme the two of them had cooked up was working. They were unlikely to get caught. They were both profiting. They had a good thing going.

That must have changed.

Marsha had commented that Jerry had turned his life around in the past few weeks. Francis said Jerry had stopped coming into the bar. He had a new girlfriend who seemed to be a good influence on him. She'd told me Jerry was going to church with her, atoning for his sins.

Could Jerry have had a change of heart? Was his scheme with Eric one of the things he wanted to atone for—and maybe confess? If so, Eric had everything to lose.

Still, it was all suspicion. I had no evidence. The only evidence was the Ford Fiesta itself that would have been damaged in the hit and run.

"Think it's in there?" Slade asked as we crept past the house.

"It's a good possibility," I said.

When I'd asked Lourdes about bringing the Thanksgiving food donation to her house, she'd said their garage door was broken and Eric had yet to fix it. But Misty had mentioned that Eric immediately had a scuffed baseboard in the office repaired.

He must have convinced Lourdes the garage door was broken so she wouldn't open it, see the front-end damage to the little Ford, and start asking questions.

"Only one way to find out," Slade said.

He slowed as we passed the house, then turned left, did a U-turn and parked at the curb.

"No windows in the garage door," he said, and killed the engine. "We'll have to go into the backyard. Houses this expensive usually have a rear door into the garage."

I climbed out of the Blazer, put my cell phone in my pocket, and left my handbag inside. If I'd known I was going on a covert op today I'd have dressed differently, but at least I wasn't wearing a skirt.

Slade got out, opened the back door and scrounged through a small tool box. He slid something into his pocket and we headed down the block.

We looked a bit mismatched but nobody seemed to notice us as we turned the corner onto Dorchester Street. We strolled past two houses and walked up Eric's driveway. As in most California neighborhoods, the rear yard of the house was enclosed by a fence. This one, because of the upscale neighborhood, was a block wall. A metal gate was positioned near the garage door. As usual, it wasn't locked.

Slade didn't hesitate. He reached over the gate, flipped the latch, and we walked through.

Eric and Lourdes, or perhaps the previous owner, had spent a fortune back there. A walkway of stamped concrete lined with low palm trees and shrubs wound through the side yard, then opened up to the rear yard. A sparkling pool was surrounded by huge rocks, palms, shrubbery, and planters. There was a massive outdoor kitchen with a stainless steel refrigerator, a huge grill, and a pizza oven. A fire pit was situated near the covered patio with tables and chairs that would accommodate a couple dozen people.

No wonder Eric had to cheat the system to afford this place.

Slade wasn't as taken with the place as I was. He was already at the door that led into the garage, working the lock with whatever he'd brought with him from his tool box. A few seconds later, the knob turned and he opened the door.

I stepped inside. Slade hit the switch by the door and a feeble light flickered on overhead.

It was a standard three-car garage with shelves on two walls that were stacked with storage bins. A mop, broom, and some cleaning supplies were beside the door that led into the house. A work bench was along another wall. The place was silent and smelled vaguely of oil and gasoline.

One car was inside, a small black Ford Fiesta bearing a California license plate that started with the number four.

"Your lucky day," Slade said.

I thought I'd be happy learning the truth. Instead, I felt kind of queasy.

"Get a picture. I'm on lookout," Slade said, then stepped outside and closed the door.

The air seemed cold and stale. I didn't want to be in

here, and immediately I was frantic to leave.

Maybe I should have called Nick.

The Ford had been backed into the garage so I circled to the front of the car. The right headlight was shattered and the fender was dented. Bits of Jerry, no doubt, were embedded in the damage.

I definitely should have called Nick.

I pulled out my cell phone and took a series of photos from several angles.

The door that led into the house flew open.

Lourdes stepped into the garage.

Chapter 13

Lourdes stood near the doorway gazing at me in the dim light. She looked as fashionable as ever, dressed in a skirt and boots, wrapped in a thick shawl. Her arms were folded and her hands were tucked in the heavy fabric, as if she were trying to warm herself. Her hair was down. I'd never realized it was so long.

I didn't realize she was home, either. Her car wasn't out front when Slade and I arrived, and I hadn't heard her pull up.

I started to panic. What was I going to say to her? How would I explain being in her garage? What if she called the police?

My mojo wasn't working so well right now.

"Hello, Dana," Lourdes said.

We stood on opposite sides of the Ford. She inched toward the rear of the car.

I'd have to tell her why I was there. But how would I break the news to her about what Eric had done? The two of them were super tight. They'd been together since high school. They'd built a solid life together, Lourdes with her ultra-fashionable home décor shop and Eric's enviable position with Mid-America. Would she even believe me?

"Eric called," Lourdes said.

She gave me an exaggerated smile, and it hit me that she was being awfully calm for someone who'd discovered a near-stranger prowling through her garage.

"He told me you dropped off the food donation," she said.

I wasn't following her, wasn't making the connection

"He called when I left the Bonita branch? And you dropped everything, and rushed home?" I asked.

She nodded. "I parked down the block and slipped into the house quietly."

My already bad mojo took a turn for the worse.

"Eric thought I'd come here," I realized.

"You were supposed to take those appraisal reports to him," Lourdes said. "But you didn't. You read them. You figured things out. And here you are, just as Eric feared."

Lourdes stopped at the back bumper. She'd hemmed me in between the Ford and the closed garage door, and cut me off from the other two exits.

I flashed on the morning Jerry had been killed when Eric had stormed into the break room demanding information from Nick. Eric had been angry. I thought he'd been annoyed by Janine's hysterical screams, but maybe I'd been wrong.

"You shouldn't have done that, Dana. You should have minded your own business and left everything alone," Lourdes said. "I will not have Eric threatened."

My conversation with Charla popped into my head. She'd told me she'd witnessed a confrontation between Jerry and a woman with long blonde hair in the alley behind Mid-America a few days before he was killed. I'd assumed it was Patricia's daughter Brooke.

Now I knew I was wrong—about everything.

"It was you," I said, and heard my voice tremble. "You argued with Jerry in the alley."

"He'd found religion, or some such nonsense, and

wanted to cleanse his conscience. He intended to confess everything. I told him not to. I told him he wasn't going to drag my Eric's name through the mud."

"You ran him down," I said.

"I gave him fair warning."

"You killed him," I said.

"He left me no choice."

Lourdes drew herself up, then pulled her arms from the folds of her shawl and pointed a 9mm pistol at me.

"And neither have you," she said.

Lourdes fired the gun. The concrete wall over my shoulder exploded, pelting me with bits of rubble.

The rear door ripped open and light flooded the garage. A silhouette filled the doorway. Slade.

Lourdes pivoted and fired. He dived to the floor. She shot at him again. He rolled to his right.

Lourdes clasped the pistol with both hands, following Slade across the floor.

There was little room for him to maneuver. She was going to kill him.

I scrambled onto the hood of the Ford, then the roof, and launched myself into Lourdes. I hit her in the back, a full body blow. We both went down hard.

Lourdes screamed. I grabbed her hands. The gun went off again. We wrestled across the floor. I rolled on top of her, pinning her down, stretching over her head to control the gun. She dug her fingernails into me. I grabbed a handful of her hair and banged her head against the concrete floor. She kicked and screamed again.

A huge black boot stepped down on her wrist. I looked up and saw Slade standing over us. He ripped the gun from her hand. I rolled aside. He flipped her around and twisted her arms behind her, then pulled a plastic wire-tie from his pocket and secured her wrists. Lourdes screamed and cursed, and struggled to get free.

I sat there dazed, then saw blood running from under Slade's T-shirt sleeve. I leaped up.

"You're hurt," I shouted.

He shrugged. "No big deal."

"She shot you. This is bad—really bad."

"A flesh wound *and* a chick fight?" Slade grinned. "Cool."

* * *

Some of the neighbors came out of their homes to stare, while others hid behind their plantation shutters and watched. All of them wanted to see what was going on.

Patrol cars blocked off the street in both directions. In front of Eric and Lourdes' house sat an ambulance, the van the crime scene guys had rolled up in, and a couple of plain white Crown Vics. A tow truck waited to haul away the Ford Fiesta.

The garage and front doors stood open. Police officers, detectives, supervisors, techs, and a photographer were going about the task of gathering evidence, conducting interviews, and documenting everything. Lourdes had been driven away in handcuffs.

We'd heard sirens within minutes of Slade subduing Lourdes. I figured a neighbor must have heard the shots and called 9-1-1.

An EMT had cleaned the gouges on my wrist left by Lourdes' fingernails and applied a bandage. I had a few aches and pains, and would likely find some bruises, but I was okay—still rattled, but okay.

Slade's flesh wound had been treated. He'd refused to go to the hospital and was now hanging out with the tow truck guys.

Nick was among the detectives working the scene. He hadn't spoken to me since he arrived.

I sat on the curb outside the house next door. At some point, I'd have to call Manny and explain why I wasn't in the office. I would have to go by Patricia's place and give her Jerry's cash. I wanted to talk to Charla and Francis, and let them know what had happened.

I wondered if Eric knew what was going on at his house. Maybe he'd been notified and was at the police station with Lourdes. Perhaps he'd been picked up, too, and was being questioned. Surely, I wasn't the only one to suspect that he had prior knowledge of Lourdes' plan to get rid of Jerry. I wondered, too, whether he would have stopped her if he'd known.

Eric was done at Mid-America, regardless. Once word got out about Jerry's inflated property values and the fraudulent loan I'd discovered, the audit team would descend and go through every document in the Bonita branch with a fine tooth comb. He'd be fired, if he didn't quit first.

Maybe that was the least of his problems right now.

Even with Eric gone, I couldn't imagine that Janine would return to the company. Not after what she'd been through. I suspected she'd recognized Lourdes behind the wheel of the Ford Fiesta but had been too afraid of her to make the accusation, understandably so.

As for Gloria, I didn't know how she hadn't figured out what Eric was up to. She'd been with the company for years. She'd heard stories. She knew how branch employees sometimes stole from the company. She knew what to watch for.

But perhaps that was part of the problem. She'd been around for so long, seen so much, been passed over for promotion so many times that she just didn't care anymore. Regardless, she might get fired.

Seemed most everybody's luck had run out.

Nick appeared in front of me. No sign of his infamous half-grin.

I didn't expect to see it.

He glared down at me and said, "I need to talk to you."

Nick didn't offer a hand to help me up, just turned and walked away. I followed him down the block and around the corner.

Nick swung around and shouted. "What the hell is the matter with you?"

His anger made me take a step back.

"You could have been killed!" A vein popped out in his forehead. "You should have called me!"

"I probably should have," I admitted.

"Why didn't you?" he demanded.

His face turned red and the vein started to throb. I'd never seen Nick this angry before.

"Tell me why!" he shouted.

I understood that he was mad, but this hadn't exactly been my best day and there was only so much I could take—especially from Nick.

"Because I didn't want to talk to you," I told him.

His anger amped up. "You nearly got yourself killed because you didn't want to talk to me?"

My anger amped up, too. "Yes! You were a complete jackass the last time I saw you! You never called, or tried to explain!"

Nick spit out a vile curse, whipped around, and paced away. He drew two big breaths, then spun back toward me.

"Are you ever going to trust me?" he asked and walked closer.

Some of his anger was gone, but not much.

"Are you?" He leaned down. "Are you ever going to believe that, sometimes, I know what's best?"

I didn't say anything.

He glared at me for a few seconds, then straightened up and backed away.

"This is about what happened back in high school, isn't it. It's so damn important for you to know what happened that now, all these years later, you can't trust my judgment." Nick flung out both arms. "Okay. Fine. It wasn't me. I didn't get Katie Jo pregnant. We never had sex. I don't know who was responsible. She didn't tell me. Whatever the circumstances, she didn't want anybody to know about it. She knew I'd be blamed. She said she was sorry. I told her not to worry, to take care of herself. I told her I could handle it."

Breath went out of me. I felt the color drain from my face.

"You could have trusted me. You could have thought I'd done the right thing. You could have thought the best of me, instead of the worst," Nick said. He backed up a step. "So at last you know. Now what?"

I had no idea.

THE END

Dear Reader,

Thanks for giving Fatal Luck a try!

If you enjoyed this book you can see how it all began in Fatal Debt, the first full-length mystery featuring Dana and Nick.

You'll probably also like my Haley Randolph mystery series available from Kensington Books in hardcover, paperback, and ebook formats. Haley is an amateur sleuth whose passion for designer handbags leads to murder.

If you're a romance reader, I also write historical fiction under the pen name Judith Stacy. You're invited to check out www.JudithStacy.com.

More information is available at www.DorothyHowellNovels.com and at my Dorothy Howell Novels fan page on Facebook. You can follow me on Twitter @DHowellNovels.

Happy reading!
Dorothy

Turn the page for a sneak peek at **Beach Bags and Burglaries**, the upcoming Haley Randolph mystery, followed by one of my favorite historical romances, **The Widow's Little Secret.**

Beach Bags and Burglaries
A Haley Randolph Mystery
Available from Kensington Books

Chapter One

"You booked us on Alcatraz," Bella said.

I gazed across the ocean at the island shrouded in fog—or maybe it was cloud cover, or haze, or smog. I don't know. This was the California coast. It could have been anything.

"I didn't book us on Alcatraz," I told her.

"Is it Skull Island?" Bella asked.

I looked again at the outline of the stone hotel and the thick vegetation on the hills rising behind it. Yeah, okay, it did kind of look like Skull Island.

Bella and I were standing in the valet line outside the Rowan Resort welcome center. We'd just caravanned from Los Angeles, our friends Marcie and Sandy following us.

Two cars had been required for the trip because each of us had brought multiple suitcases, garment bags, totes, and duffels, all of which were absolutely necessary—I mean, jeez, we were staying a whole week.

We were all dressed in the latest resort wear. I had maxed out an impressive number of credit cards for the occasion.

I was willing to do more, of course. *Vogue* magazine had declared the Sea Vixen—a gorgeous polka dot beach tote—the *it* bag of the season, and I absolutely had to have one. In the last few days I'd scoured every high-end shop in L.A. and hadn't located one. It was majorly disappointing, but no way was I giving up the search.

Sandy jumped out of Marcie's car, while Marcie sat behind the wheel fiddling with her cell phone.

"Wow, Haley, this is totally awesome," Sandy said. "I can't wait to get there!"

According to the itinerary provided by the travel agent, we would relax in the comfort of the VIP lounge until we were picked up by a limo and driven to a helicopter for the flight to our all-expense-paid vacation at one of the world's most exclusive locations. The Rowan Resort catered to the every whim of A-list celebrities, royalty, and millionaires, offering privacy and seclusion amid ultra luxurious accommodations.

So you might be wondering why I, Haley Randolph, a part-time salesclerk at the I-don't-tell-anyone-I-work-there Holt's Department Store—although I'm quick to mention my way cool job as an event planner at L.A. Affairs—could afford such a fantastic vacation for not only myself but my three BFFs. Honestly, the whole thing was a bit hazy to me, too.

Not long ago I won a contest at Holt's—long story—and the grand prize was a seven-day cruise. I'd also won yet another contest at Holt's—again, long story—but the so-called prize required that I work at the Holt's corporate office, something I had no interest in doing, so I'd put that whole thing on ignore.

Anyway, when I called the travel agency to ask about booking the cruise, I was told the prize had been upgraded to a week at the Rowan Resort, which was cooler than cool, of course, and that absolutely anything and everything was mine for the asking.

I had no idea why the prize had been changed, but I rolled with it.

Seeing no reason not to take advantage of the situation, I immediately asked my three BFFs to come with me. I mean, really, who else would I invite?

Marcie and I had been friends forever. We're both twenty-four years old, but that's where any resemblance ended. She was short and a blonde. I was a five-foot-nine brunette.

We could pass for a ventriloquist act.

I'd met Bella—standing side by side we looked like piano keys—and Sandy—a redhead whose mother had, apparently, identified a little too closely with Olivia Newton-John in *Grease*—about a year ago when I took the salesclerk job at Holt's.

So you also might be wondering why I didn't have a boyfriend to take with me on this fabulous vacation. Actually, I had a boyfriend. His name was Ty Cameron. Ty was the fifth generation in his family to run the chain of Holt's Department Stores. He was handsome, smart, and generous, and he looked great in an Armani suit.

We broke up.

I'm not thinking about that now. I'm on vacation.

An army of valets swarmed around our cars—even though Marcie's Toyota and my Honda weren't the Jaguars, Porsches, and Mercedes they were used to seeing here at the welcome center—as a woman in a burgundy suit greeted us. A gold name tag that read MILLICENT, HOSTESS was pinned to her lapel.

"Welcome," she cooed. "How was your drive, Miss Randolph?"

I had no idea how she knew who I was. Maybe

searching guest info on the Internet was part of the service.

"Is Brad Pitt here? I saw online that he was here," Sandy said. "Oh my God, I'd die if I saw Brad Pitt."

Millicent gave Sandy an indulgent smile, then ignored her comment and gestured toward the doors of the welcome center. "Your lounge is waiting."

Bella cast another glance at the island. "We've got to fly to that place?"

"The Rowan Resort is a quick flight—"

Millicent stopped midsentence and did a double-take at Bella's hair.

That happens a lot.

Bella's goal was to be a hairdresser to the stars—she worked at Holt's to save for beauty school—and she practiced on her own hair. Today, in keeping with the tropical theme of our vacation, she'd styled a dolphin atop her head.

Millicent recovered and said, "It's a quick flight in one of our luxury helicopters."

"There's no bridge?" Bella asked.

Millicent displayed yet another indulgent smile. "The island is miles from the mainland. A bridge across that expanse of the Pacific Ocean is an engineering impossibility."

"What about one of those ferry boats?" Bella asked.

"A ferry once took guests and family members back and forth, but that was many years ago," Millicent explained. "Now our guests fly in using one of our helicopters."

"That's the only way to get on and off that island?" Bella asked.

Millicent gave her an I-give-excellent-customer-service-no-matter-what smile, then said, "A dock is located on the north side of the island where supply boats come in. But you needn't concern yourself with them. Our security personnel are on duty at the dock and helipad, ensuring complete privacy during your stay."

Millicent didn't hang around to answer more questions. She headed inside, leaving us to follow.

"Haley, this is so cool. We're going to see all kinds of celebrities, I just know it," Sandy said as she hurried past me.

Bella threw another look at the island, then followed Sandy inside.

Marcie finally got out of her car, her gaze still glued to her cell phone.

"Did he text you?" I asked.

She looked up. "What? Oh. Oh, no. It's—it's something else."

We walked inside the welcome center, a large room that looked as if somebody's great-grandmother had decorated it. It was filled with statues, paintings, and if-you-weigh-more-than-eighty-pounds-don't-sit-here furniture.

My Sea Vixen beach bag would have definitely brightened up the place.

Millicent held open a door on our right and said, "Your lounge."

We filed inside. The dimly lit room was cool and quiet. Accent lighting beamed down on black-and-white photos mounted on the walls. Several seating groups were scattered around. A guy in a burgundy vest and tie stood behind a bar, and a cart filled with food was nearby.

A man and woman had claimed the comfy chairs closest to the bar. They were gray-haired, a little thick around the middle. Definitely not celebrities. More like a couple whose kids had treated them to the trip of a lifetime for their wedding anniversary.

Marcie, Sandy, Bella, and I sat down, and the bartender was on us immediately. He rolled the food cart over and took our drink orders.

"That's him," Marcie said, nodding toward one of the photos on the wall. "That's Sidney Rowan. I saw his picture on the Internet. He bought the mansion and the island back in the day, and later it was turned into a hotel and resort."

In the photo, which from the depicted clothing, hair, and makeup looked like it had been taken a few decades ago, Sidney Rowan had on a tuxedo and stood between two young women decked out in evening attire. He was tall, thin, and handsome in an old-school way, and kind of looked like that guy who danced all the time in those black-and-white movies.

"Yes, that's right," Millicent said, suddenly popping up in front of us. "Mr. Rowan amassed an empire that reached every corner of the globe, then purchased his home on the island for occasions when he needed to get away from it all."

The bartender served our drinks, and we loaded our plates with delicacies from the buffet cart.

"Looks like he knew all the big stars back then," Sandy said, pointing to the photographs.

"That's Elizabeth Taylor," Bella said. "How old is that guy?"

"He's a recluse," said the woman seated near the bar. "He hasn't been seen in decades. Nobody knows if he's even alive now."

Millicent smiled her I'm-ignoring-that-comment smile and said, "The main structure was built in the thirties. After Mr. Rowan purchased it in the sixties, additions were made to accommodate his growing family, and guest bungalows were built for his many friends and business associates. Receiving an invitation to the island was highly prized."

Millicent's comments started to sound like a history lesson. I drifted off.

That happens a lot.

I got yanked back into reality when Marcie nudged me with her elbow.

"It's been all over the Internet," she whispered.

Something was all over the Internet?

"They're trying to keep it quiet," she said, "but bloggers and celebrity sites are making a big deal out of it."

I've been kind of out of the loop for a while.

"It's nothing," Millicent said. She was definitely in backpedal mode. "Speculation and conjecture, unfortunately, broadcast by people who have no actual knowledge of the event or the facts."

"That girl might be dead," insisted the woman near the bar. "Nobody just disappears—not off of an island. The whole thing is suspicious and very mysterious. She might even have been murdered."

"Was she a celebrity?" Sandy asked.

"Murdered?" Bella demanded. "A girl on that island was murdered?"

"Thank goodness it wasn't Jennifer Aniston," Sandy said. "I love Jennifer Aniston."

"She was an employee," Millicent said, as if that somehow made her possible death okay. "And nothing definite has been determined. She's missing. That's all. There's no reason to suspect foul play."

"The police were called in. The island was searched. They can't find her," the woman declared.

"There's no reason to worry," Millicent insisted. "This happened only yesterday."

"Yesterday?" Bella echoed. She waved to the bartender. "Bring me a bourbon on the rocks—make it a double."

"Does JLo know about this?" Sandy asked. "I read in *People* that she comes to the resort a lot."

"There's absolutely nothing to be alarmed about," Millicent said.

"Nothing to be alarmed about?" the woman exclaimed. "Somebody may have died!"

"Enough!" Her husband pushed to his feet. "It's nothing but gossip. I'm not listening to another word of this."

"But, Harvey—"

"Get our limo," he barked at Millicent. "Come along, Geraldine. We're going to the island, and I don't want to hear any more of this nonsense."

Millicent scurried to a door at the rear of the room and flung it open. Sunlight poured inside.

"You ladies can remain here as long as you'd like," she said. "Your limo will take you to the helicopter at your convenience."

The couple disappeared out the door. Millicent followed.

"Is that true?" Bella asked. "Did somebody really go missing, maybe get murdered out there?"

"Nobody knows for sure," Marcie said. "Right now it's just a lot of speculation."

"And it wasn't a celebrity," Sandy added. "Wow, I wonder if that old guy who owns the resort knows about this? I mean, if he's not dead, too."

I kept up on celebrity news, and nearly everybody on the planet knew there had been all kinds of rumors for years about Sidney Rowan. He'd been labeled an eccentric recluse who wielded power over his global, multi-billion-dollar empire from a chalet in Switzerland, a Buddhist temple in Nepal, a penthouse in Las Vegas—all sorts of places. There had been reported sightings of him in Paris, Belize, Moscow, most everywhere. But none of them had been confirmed by a legitimate news source— nor had anyone proved whether the old geezer was really alive or dead.

"I don't like hearing about dead people when I'm on vacay. Gives me the heebie-jeebies," Bella said. "Plus, I'm not loving that whole stuck-on-an-island thing, especially with all those bushes and trees and snakes and big bugs, and who knows what else."

"Are you sure you want to go to the resort?" I asked.

Bella stewed for a minute, then stood up.

"Yeah, I'll go," she said. "But if we get captured by some psycho jungle tribe like you see in the movies and they demand a virgin sacrifice, we're in big trouble."

Nobody disagreed.

Millicent came into the lounge, and I told her we were ready to leave. She darted outside again.

"Hang on a second," I said as we headed for the door. "Remember our pact?"

The four of us formed a circle, and I could see that we were all thinking over the decision we'd made when we undertook this trip.

Things hadn't been great for any of us, dating wise. Marcie had a first date with a guy who seemed great but hadn't bothered to tweet, text, call, e-mail, or Facebook her since that night. Sandy's tattoo artist boyfriend had left on sabbatical without her. Bella wasn't all that anxious to get involved with a man, fearing he'd distract her from saving for beauty school. I, course, had just broken up with my official boyfriend, Ty.

"No men, and no men-talk," I said. "No complaining, no whining, no moaning about the men in our lives. This is a girl trip. We're going to relax, have fun, enjoy ourselves, and not waste our emotion, time, and effort on them. Agreed?"

"You bet," Marcie said.

"Sounds good to me," Sandy said.

"I got no problem with it," Bella said. "But I brought my lucky panties, just in case."

Bella and Sandy headed out the door, but Marcie stayed put.

"Have you seen the latest news?" she asked.

I got a weird feeling.

"It's all over the Internet," she repeated.

My weird feeling got weirder.

"That girl who's gone missing at the resort?" Marcie gestured to her phone. "They found her driver's license and cell phone at the top of the cliffs on the back side of the island. Bloggers are speculating that she either jumped—or was pushed. She really might have been murdered."

Oh, crap.

In the mood for a little romance?

You'll find it in the light, funny historical romance set in 1877 Nevada

The Widow's Little Secret

Written under Dorothy's pen name, Judith Stacy

With a baby coming and her business failing, Mattie Ingram wonders what else could possibly happen. She finds out when the father of her child, U.S. Marshal Jared McQuaid, insists on becoming a permanent part of her life.

But if Jared thinks that one night of passion gives him the right to a lifetime commitment, he had better think again!

The Widow's Little Secret
By Judith Stacy
Available from Harlequin Historicals in paperback and
e-book formats

Chapter One

Nevada, 1877

It just wasn't right, being envious of a dead man. Still, that's how Jared McQuaid felt sitting on the hotel porch, watching the funeral procession roll by.

He glanced down at the *Stanford Gazette* on his lap. The headline announced the untimely death of Del Ingram, and the front page article extolled the man's many virtues.

A knot formed in Jared's stomach. What were the chances? He'd showed up in this town just today and read the obituary of a man he'd grown up with miles and miles from here. A man he hadn't thought of in years.

According to the newspaper, Ingram had died from a fall. Jared had figured ol' Del was more likely to have been killed by a jealous husband, an irate wife or a poker player with an eye for cheaters.

Not so, according to the newspaper. Del had made something of himself here in Stanford. Owner of a restaurant, a solid citizen with a sterling reputation, he'd had a life any man would envy.

Jared touched his hand to the U.S. Marshal's badge pinned to his vest beneath his coat. Seemed he and his boyhood friend had taken very different roads when they'd parted company some fifteen years ago. This wasn't the man Jared remembered. But maybe Del had changed.

Jared sure as hell had.

The rocker creaked as Jared leaned back and watched from beneath the brim of his black Stetson as the funeral procession passed by. Matched sorrels pulled the wagon bearing the coffin, their hoofs stirring up little swirls of dust. Two dozen mourners followed, all dressed in black, their somber faces flushed from the raw March wind.

Jared glanced west. Charcoal clouds hung over the Sierra Nevadas, blocking out what was left of the day's sunlight. He had nothing to do, no place to go, no one to talk to until morning when he would relieve Stanford's sheriff of his two prisoners and head to Carson City. Jared may as well pay his respects to Del Ingram, even though he'd never especially liked him.

A few people glanced at Jared as he fell into step behind the mourners. One woman eyed the Colt .45 strapped to his hip and the badge on his chest when the wind whipped open his coat. She chanced a look at his face, then turned away, wondering, he was sure, who he was and why he was here.

Jared found himself on the receiving end of a hundred such looks nearly every time he came to a town like this. Not that he blamed anyone, of course. He'd arrive one day, eat supper alone in some restaurant, sleep in a nameless hotel, then take custody of his prisoners the following morning and disappear.

And those were his good days. Most of the time he

was on the trail, sleeping in the saddle, eating jerky and cold beans, hunting down some rabble-rouser who'd broken the law.

He was used to both—the life and the looks he got. Jared had been a marshal for nearly ten years now.

At the cemetery on the edge of town, six men unloaded the coffin from the wagon. Del Ingram's final resting place was deep; freshly turned earth lay beside it.

Reverend Harris stepped to the foot of the grave, yanked his black, wide-brimmed hat over the tufts of his gray hair and struggled to hold open the fluttering pages of his Bible. The townsfolk gathered in a close knot, straining to hear the reverend's words. Jared moved off to one side, uncomfortable among the mourners.

As was his custom, Jared's gaze moved from face to face, sizing up each person assembled there. He was good at it. It had saved his life a time or two.

From all appearances, everyone who was anyone in the town of Stanford was assembled to mourn Del's passing. They all looked prosperous, in dress and in manner. Jared spotted the mayor and his wife; he'd met the man earlier in the sheriff's office. Sheriff Hickert wasn't present, but Jared hadn't expected him to be. He was nursing a nasty leg wound from the shoot-out that had garnered the two prisoners Jared was transporting tomorrow.

The gathering shifted as Reverend Harris reached for the woman standing in front of him. Jared's stomach bottomed out.

"Damn…"

The widow. Del's widow. Jared felt like he'd been sucker-punched in the gut.

He didn't know how Ingram had acquired a

prosperous business, a good home, a sterling reputation—and he sure as hell couldn't imagine how he'd found himself such a fine-looking wife.

Even in her mourning dress she looked fit and shapely. She'd draped a black lace scarf over her head, but tendrils of her brown hair escaped in the wind and blew across her pale cheeks. She stood stiff and straight, her full lips pressed tightly together as she gazed past the reverend to some point on the distant horizon.

Jared thought she looked brave, determined not to break down. He wondered if she'd fully accepted the sudden loss of her husband, dead not quite two days now. He'd seen that happen before, where a long time passed before reality set in—and only then did loved ones fall to pieces.

Who would be there to hold Mrs. Del Ingram when that happened? Jared wondered. He wondered, too, why the thought bothered him so much.

He recalled the newspaper article he'd read, and remembered no mention of Ingram having any children. Indeed, no little ones hung on Mrs. Ingram's skirt, sniffling, reaching up to her. Jared found that troubling. The widow was truly alone now, it seemed, without even a child to comfort her.

"Let us pray," Reverend Harris called.

As heads bowed, Jared pulled out the newspaper, which he'd crammed into his pocket, and searched for the widow's name. Matilda. "Mattie," the mayor's wife had called her in a quote.

He turned to her again. His breath caught. Mattie Ingram hadn't bowed her head for the prayer. She was looking straight at him.

Their gazes met and held. She didn't blink, didn't

falter, didn't hesitate, just looked at him long and hard, with the biggest, brownest eyes he'd ever seen.

Heat flared in Jared's belly, spreading outward, weakening his knees and making his heart thump harder in his chest.

"Amen," the reverend intoned.

"Amen," the gathering echoed.

Only then did Mattie turn away. Flushed, Jared pushed back his coat to welcome the chilly wind.

He watched her, silently willing her to turn toward him again. But she didn't. Rigid, restrained, Mattie accepted condolences, then headed back toward town, with the other mourners crowded around her.

Standing beside the mound of dirt at Ingram's grave, Jared followed her with his gaze, the bustle under her dark dress swaying, the vision of her deep brown eyes still boring into him. Finally, she disappeared from sight. Jared headed for the closest saloon.

Almost nobody was inside the Lady Luck when Jared passed through the bat-wing doors. Two men stood at the bar; the gaming tables were empty.

"Pretty quiet in here," Jared said to the bartender.

"Everybody's paying their respects," he said, and nodded outside, "down at Mrs. Ingram's place."

Jared should have known that. The mourners would gather at the widow's house, eat the food they'd brought, and talk one final time about the departed.

Jared leaned his elbow on the bar. Had he been on the trail so long he'd forgotten how civilized people acted?

Over the next few hours the saloon filled with men, drinks flowed and the noise level rose. Everybody who came in had something to say about Del Ingram. Jared stood at the bar sipping his drink, trying to block it out. By the time he'd finished his fourth beer he'd heard all the tributes he could stand to hear about the man he remembered to be a first-rate scalawag, the man these townsfolk admired so much.

Outside, the cold wind whipped around Jared as he headed down the boardwalk toward the hotel. It was dark now. The town had closed up for the night.

But when he reached the hotel, Jared kept walking. He didn't stop until he got to the edge of town, to the sturdy house with the picket fence he'd read about in the newspaper. The Ingram home.

And a fine home it was. Neat, clean, well built. A house fit for one of Stanford's most prosperous citizens.

The front door opened and a woman stepped onto the porch, outlined by the glowing lamplight behind her. Jared's heart lurched. Was it her? Was it Mattie?

The woman pulled two small children out of the house behind her and shut the door. Disappointment caused Jared's shoulders to sag a little. He nodded politely to the woman when she passed him on her way back to town.

Minutes dragged by while Jared stood at the end of the boardwalk, looking at the Ingram home. He didn't want to go inside and hear anyone else talk about what a fine man Del was; Jared had had his fill of that already.

He muttered a little curse directed at himself. What kind of man was he, thinking ill of the dead? Had he forgotten all the good manners he'd once prided himself on?

Slowly, he nodded in the darkness. His solitary life on the trail, hunting down criminals, hauling them in for trial, had taken its toll.

The decent thing to do was go pay his respects to the

widow of the man he'd grown up with. Del had made something of his life and he deserved all the things being said about him. Jared would go into that house and say something nice about him. It was the right thing to do.

And he'd get to see Mattie Ingram again.

Jared crossed the road, passed through the little gate outside the house and stepped up onto the porch. He paused for a moment before he knocked and brushed off his trousers, then took off his hat and smoothed down his dark hair, glad he'd taken a bath and gotten a haircut this afternoon.

He rapped his knuckles against the door, then waited, waited and waited some more before it opened. He'd expected to find the reverend's wife greeting mourners, but instead Jared found himself face-to-face with the widow herself. A long moment dragged by while he just looked at her. When Jared finally came to his senses, he clasped his hat against his chest and tried to think of something to say.

"Mrs. Ingram? My name is Jared McQuaid. I'm— I'm real sorry about your husband."

She stepped back without really looking at him, and opened the door wider. "Won't you come in?"

He followed her down a little hallway, past a near parlor, to the kitchen at the rear of the house. The room was warm and comfortable. A cook stove and cupboards were at one end, a sideboard and a table and chairs at the other. All manner of food—or what was left of it— covered the table. Jared's steps slowed. No one else was in the house. Had he intruded, when he'd intended to comfort?

"Is it too late to come calling?" he asked.

"No," she said simply, and turned toward the

---

cupboard. "I'll get you something to eat."

Jared watched her skirt swirl, and glimpsed her white ruffled petticoat, then studied her backside as she stretched up and retrieved a plate from the top shelf of the cupboard.

He muttered a silent curse at himself for admiring Del's widow.

"Your husband and I grew up together," Jared said, as he shrugged out of his coat and laid his hat aside.

Mattie didn't answer, just turned again and began filling the plate from the dishes on the table.

"We went to school together," Jared said, feeling the need to say something. He took a step closer. "I'm a U.S. Marshal, just in town for today. I'm leaving in the morning. I read about Del in the newspaper."

Silence filled the house as Mattie heaped food on the plate, and Jared pulled at the back of his neck.

"So, while I was here I wanted to tell you how sorry I am that Del's passed on," he said. "He was a good man. Everybody in town speaks highly of him."

Though Jared didn't understand it, it was true. And regardless of what he thought about Del Ingram, this was his wife, the woman who loved him. She'd married him, lain with him, walked through life with him. The least Jared could do was think of something nice to say.

"Fact is," Jared said. "I never heard so many kind things said about one man before. I was down at the Lady Luck just now and Del was all anybody talked about."

A little gasp echoed in the kitchen, and Jared saw Mattie press her hand against her lips. Damn it, what was he thinking, mentioning that he'd been at the saloon? That wasn't what women liked to hear from strangers in their home.

Jared pushed his fingers through his hair. "The mayor … the mayor had nice things to say, too."

She dropped the plate she'd been preparing and leaned forward, bracing her hand on the table. Little sniffles filled the room.

Good Lord, he'd made her cry. Jared stared at her slumping shoulders as she tried bravely to stand upright. He wanted to go to her, take her in his arms, comfort her. But should he? He didn't even know her.

He wasn't sure what to do but keep talking.

"The newspaper article about Del was just about the most glowing report I'd ever read. And that eulogy, that was something, all right."

A sob tore from her lips and her whole body quivered. Jared stepped closer until he stood mere inches away.

He wanted to hold her. Oh, he wanted to hold her like he'd never wanted to hold another thing in his life. She looked so frail and helpless; her sobs sounded so pitiful. He wanted to press her against his chest and let her cry, keep her in his arms until her tears stopped.

"Your husband was a good man. He was well respected, and honest, and hardworking," Jared said softly. "You've every right to be upset, Mrs. Ingram."

"Don't call me that!"

Mattie swung around, hot anger boiling inside her. She drew back her fist and struck Jared in the chest.

"Don't ever call me by that name again!" she screamed. "He was a bastard! A lying, conniving bastard!"

Mattie braced one hand against the table to keep herself up, unable to hold the words inside any longer. She'd done that for nearly two days now, and she couldn't contain them another minute.

"I've had to pretend since he died—pretend that he was a good man, pretend that everything said about him was the truth." A sob tore from her lips. "But none of it is true. None of it!"

"Mrs. Ingram—Mattie—maybe you should—"

She batted away Jared's hand when he reached for her. "It was a lie. Right from the beginning. Del never loved me."

Jared eased closer. "Things might seem that way now because you're upset, but—"

"He told me! Just before he died!" Another wave of tears poured down Mattie's cheeks.

Jared frowned. "He told you he never loved you?"

Mattie nodded, the hurt and humiliation throbbing in her chest. "He fell off the roof and was injured badly. He knew he was going to die. So he told me. He told me everything. How he followed another woman here to Stanford because he was in love with her. How he couldn't have her because she was marrying someone else. How he married me because I had a restaurant, a good home, a good reputation, money."

"Son of a ..."

Mattie gulped, her strength draining away. She latched on to Jared's arms, gazing up at him. "He just used me," she whispered.

Mattie fell against him, sobbing, the pain too great to bear alone. She felt big arms close around her. She snuggled deeper against his hard chest.

With a sharp, ragged breath she lifted her head and gazed up at Jared. "I went to the bank today. My account was nearly empty. He'd taken my money, gambled it away, most likely. Lord knows he never worked a day since I married him. I had to use the last dollar I have in this world to bury him!"

She fell into racking sobs again and slumped against Jared's chest. Gently, he stroked his fingers down her back, fearing Mattie was on the verge of all-out hysteria.

"You need the doctor," he said. "He can—"

"No!" Mattie pulled away. "No, don't get the doctor. Don't get *anyone*. I don't want people to know how stupid I was, how I let myself be swept off my feet by a man I hardly knew. Everyone said I shouldn't marry him, but I wouldn't listen. I believed that he loved me. I don't want the whole town to know what a fool I was."

Jared shook his head. "Mattie, you're too upset. You need—"

"—to forget," she said, wiping away her tears with the back of her hand. "I need to forget."

Jared froze as she gazed up at him. The look on her face sent a warm tremor through him.

"Make me forget," she whispered.

Mattie came fully against him and rose on her toes, pressing her lips to his throat. "Please ... make me forget."

"Now, just a minute." Jared caught her arms and tried to ease her away. "You're not thinking clear."

"I don't want to think clear. I don't want to think at all," she said, and slid her palm across his chest.

He backed up, but she moved with him. "You don't mean that."

She meant it. With all her heart and soul she meant it. She ached deep inside. She wanted it to go away. She wanted to feel something different.

And who better to do that with than this stranger, who'd be gone in the morning?

Mattie circled her arms around his neck and pressed her lips to his. He pulled away.

"We were married for nearly a year, but he hadn't touched me in months—months!" she said. "Please. I can't lie alone in that bed tonight. I just can't."

Jared hesitated, studying her in the dim light.

"You can do it, can't you?" she asked. "You can make me forget?"

"Damn right I can," he said. "But that's not the point."

"What's wrong with it?" she asked. "I'm not a married woman … not anymore."

"I know, but—"

"I want this," she whispered. "Don't make me plead with you."

"But …"

Mattie stepped away and held out her hand to him. "Please, just make me forget."

He didn't move, not for a long minute. Then, finally, Jared reached for her hand.

CPSIA information can be obtained at www.ICGtesting.com
Printed in the USA
LVOW07s0413050416

482093LV00002B/373/P